DATE DUE

The Secret Zoo

SECRETS AND SHADOWS

THE SECRET ZOO

SECRETS AND SHADOWS

BRYAN CHICK

GREENWILLOW BOOKS
An Imprint of HarperCollinsPublishers

The Secret Zoo: Secrets and Shadows
Copyright © 2011 by Bryan Chick

All rights reserved. No part of this book may be used or reproduced in any manner whatsoever without written permission except in the case of brief quotations embodied in critical articles and reviews. Printed in the United States of America. For information address HarperCollins Children's Books, a division of HarperCollins Publishers, 10 East 53rd Street, New York, NY 10022.

www.harpercollinschildrens.com

The text of this book is set in 10 1/2-point Arrus BT
Book design by Paul Zakris

Library of Congress Cataloging-in-Publication Data
Chick, Bryan.
The secret zoo : secrets and shadows / by Bryan Chick.
p. cm.
"Greenwillow Books."
Summary: Noah and his friends in the Secret Society join forces with four teens known as the Descenders to try to protect the Secret Zoo hidden behind the Clarksville City Zoo from monstrous sasquatches and the evil Shadowist.
ISBN 978-0-06-198925-4 (trade bdg.)
[1. Mystery and detective stories. 2. Zoos—Fiction. 3. Zoo animals—Fiction. 4. Sasquatch—Fiction. 5. Friendship—Fiction.] I. Title. II. Title: Secrets and shadows.
PZ7.C4336Se 2011   [Fic]—dc22   2010017221

11 12 13 14 15 LP/RRDB 10 9 8 7 6 5 4 3 2 1
First Edition

GREENWILLOW BOOKS

FOR THE KIDS AT WATERFORD KNUDSEN
AND THEIR LIBRARIAN, SANDY FELTZER,
WHO FIRST OPENED THE SECRET ZOO

❧ PRELUDE ❧

THE REQUEST

"You ready for this?"

Noah's eyes dropped to the note in his hands. He scanned the page and returned his attention to the Action Scouts. The four friends were huddled on Noah's bedroom floor, sitting cross-legged. They'd just stepped in from the cold outdoors, so they were still wearing their winter headgear: Richie, his cap with the oversized pom-pom; Ella, her big pink earmuffs; Megan, her sporty fleece headband; and Noah, his red hunting cap that he'd discovered in the Secret Zoo. Noah's eyes met Ella's, then Richie's, and finally Megan's.

Richie responded with a quick nod, sending shivers through the pom-pom on his cap.

Noah held out the note that Marlo, the tiny kingfisher from the Clarksville Zoo, had delivered to them just minutes ago in their tree fort. He coughed into his fist and began to read.

> *Dearest Action Scouts,*
>
> *I'm afraid I have regrettable news. In the struggle to hunt down the sasquatches that fled the Dark Lands, our Secret Society has met with complete failure. The sasquatches have hidden in different sectors. We don't know where they are or what they're capable of. I cannot write more about this here except to say that there are elements concerning the Secret Zoo that I have alluded to but never fully explained to you.*
>
> *Tomorrow after school, can you meet with Tank and me in PizZOOria, the large cafeteria in the Clarksville Zoo? Tank and I will cross to the Outside and await your arrival. Our meeting will be brief. We have a proposition for you. Our only requirement is that you arrive with an open mind.*
>
> *Sincerely,*
> *Mr. Darby*

Noah folded the note and turned his attention to his friends. "Well?" he said. "What do you make of that?"

For a moment, no one spoke. At last, Richie said, "It sounds like they need our help."

"Yeah," Noah said. "But are we ready to give it? I mean . . . *really* give it?" It had, after all, been only two weeks since Noah's sister, Megan, had been rescued from the Secret Zoo.

"I don't know," Richie answered. He pushed up his big eyeglasses. "Let's meet Mr. Darby and hear what he has to say."

"I agree," Megan said.

Ella nodded.

"Okay," said Noah. "After school. Tomorrow. Marlo will be back in the morning. I'll send our reply then."

The scouts stared at one another in silence. Then Noah folded the note and set it on his nightstand.

On their dark walk home from Noah and Megan's house, Richie and Ella couldn't stop talking about the note from Mr. Darby. He was the leader of the Secret Society, a band of humans and animals living side by side in a magical kingdom that existed behind the walls of their local zoo. As the two scouts rushed through their dark neighborhood streets, Ella suddenly halted and swung out her arm, thumping Richie across his chest.

"Ow!" Richie said. "What are you—"

"Quiet, Richie—I mean it!"

In the silent intersection, the two of them stood perfectly still. Ella looked out at the dark surroundings: a street in every direction; houses on corner lots; empty cars parked along curbs.

"I saw something," she whispered. "Something . . . something moving."

"Like what?" Richie asked with concern. Then a gleam of hope flashed across his face. "Like . . . a chipmunk?"

Ella glanced at him. "Someone's watching us."

Richie's face sank with such force that Ella half expected his eyes, ears, and nose to tumble to the ground and lie there like Mr. Potato Head pieces. He kept his voice to a whisper. "What? Seriously, where?"

Ella directed a finger across the street to a yard whose densely planted spruce trees grew higher than the surrounding telephone poles. A dark blur moved from the shadow of one spruce into the shadow of another.

Keeping perfectly still, Ella said, "Did you see that?"

"Yes. What was it?"

After a moment of silence, Ella delivered the simple truth. "It was him."

Every cell in Richie's body froze. Finally, he said, "If by *him*, you mean Mr. Peters, checking his mail, then I'm cool with that. But if you're talking about—"

"It's the same guy I saw standing in your neighbor's yard, Richie, the night I woke you up to sneak into the zoo. And it's the same guy Tank was talking about—the man who lives in the shadows—who *is* the shadows."

Ella recalled their first meeting with Tank, the enormous Clarksville Zoo security guard formally known as Mr. Pangbourne. Her memory restored an image of the man looming above the scouts, his bald head shining, his muscular arms crossed as he spoke for the first time of the Shadowist—the near-mythical man who was hunting for the Secret Zoo.

Now the scouts stared into the shadows of the yard. Besides swaying branches, there was no movement. If a man had been there, he was gone now.

"C'mon," Ella said. "Let's get out of here."

And the two of them did. As fast as they could.

❦ CHAPTER 1 ❧
A Decision at PizZOOria

The following morning, Marlo showed up at Noah's window as promised, and Noah gave the tiny blue bird a note that simply read, "See you after school." Clutching the paper in his little talons, Marlo flew across Noah's yard, which backed against the Clarksville Zoo, then darted over the high wall. Within minutes, the kingfisher would find a hidden tunnel to the Secret Zoo, pass through it, and deliver the note to Mr. Darby.

At three-thirty that afternoon, the scouts headed to PizZOOria. They had more than two hours before any of their parents would return home from work—plenty of time, since their houses were next to the zoo. On the way, Ella and Richie shared again their account of someone watching them from the shadows on their walk home. Megan and Noah listened to it all, just as frightened as they had been the first time.

At PizZOOria, the foursome pushed through the big double doors and walked in side by side. Noah imagined how they must have looked: steadfast and purposeful, like soldiers marching into battle.

Tank and Mr. Darby were sitting at a booth. Mr. Darby was drinking something from a plastic concession cup shaped like a hippo. The cup looked out of place against Mr. Darby's long gray beard and serious demeanor. Mr. Darby had traded his usual velvet trench coat for common pants and a sweater. Perched on his nose were his regular sunglasses, concealing his eyes. Tank was eating. He'd passed on PizZOOria's traditional dish in favor of something greasier. In front of him was a wobbly stack of cheeseburgers and a mountain of French fries. His enormous arms bulged as he fed fries into his mouth.

Mr. Darby beamed as the scouts approached. He rose to his feet, saying, "My dear scouts!" The old man swept his arm toward the booth, inviting them to take a seat.

The children plopped down, shaking the booth and almost toppling Tank's tower of cheeseburgers.

"Tank!" Richie said. "Good to see you . . . but even better to see your fries. Mind if I—?"

With a wink, Tank said, "Help yourself, bub."

Noah turned to Mr. Darby and said, "Good to see you again."

"Indeed it is," the old man replied.

Tank nodded, winked again, and devoured half a cheeseburger with a single bite.

"First things first," Ella said. She leaned across the booth toward Mr. Darby. "Last night, Richie and I, we saw that guy in our neighborhood again—that shadow dude."

Mr. Darby lifted his eyebrows above his sunglasses. "What?"

In an attempt to say, "It's true," Richie said, "Did-poo" and sprayed chewed-up potatoes into the air.

Megan adjusted her glasses and spoke. "He followed them home."

Mr. Darby frowned. "And how can you be certain it was"—he reduced his voice to a whisper—"him? How can you know?"

Ella said, "Well, not too many of our neighbors run around their yards at night in trench coats and funky-looking hats."

Mr. Darby said nothing, but he and Tank shared an uneasy glance.

"I thaw that," Richie said as he moved in for another sloppy helping of fries. His hand bumped Tank's and seemed puny and pale against the big man's dark-skinned mass of knuckles.

"Yeah," Noah said. "I saw it, too. If there's any chance that we might be in some kind of trouble, you guys need to tell us."

"You're right," Mr. Darby said. "You need to know all that we know about the Shadowist—that is certain. However, this is not the time or place—which leads in nicely to why I asked the four of you here."

"Go ahead," said Noah.

"When will it be safe for the four of you to come back?"

"To the Secret Zoo?" Megan asked. "I'm not so sure I ever want to see that place again!"

"Understandable, given your past plight, dear Megan." Mr. Darby was referring to the three weeks she'd spent trapped in the Dark Lands, a forbidden land at the edge of the City of Species inside the Secret Zoo. "Do you all feel the same way?"

The scouts glanced at one another. They kept silent.

"Perhaps you would consider a single trip back, yes? Then we can talk about this matter further. After you cross over, Tank and I will arrange for an escort to see you back safely to the City of Species."

"An escort?" Ella said.

"Yes, we'll arrange guides to see you across the sector."

Knowing that sectors were different regions of terrain inside the Secret Zoo, Noah asked, "What exhibit do you want us to enter through?"

Tank cut in. "Metr-APE-olis. Isn't that what we're thinking, Mr. D?"

Mr. Darby nodded. "Your entire commitment will be less than two hours. What do you say?"

The scouts traded a look of uncertainty, and then all eyes settled on Noah. After a moment, Noah said, "Okay. We can check it out, at least."

"Excellent!" Mr. Darby clapped his hands and rubbed his palms together. "What day will you come?"

After waiting for Richie to free up enough space in his mouth to talk, the scouts decided on Saturday morning, which was two days away, as long as they could clear it with their parents. They decided on eight o'clock, an hour before the zoo opened.

"Very well! I'll instruct the zoo guards to allow the four of you into the zoo early." Mr. Darby stood up along with Tank.

"But how do we get inside?" Megan said. "At Metr-APE-olis, how do we get in?"

"Just find Daisy," Tank said. "She'll know what to do."

Mr. Darby added, "Your parents permitting, we'll see

the four of you Saturday." He tipped his head, and he and Tank left through the double doors.

"That's it, then," Noah said.

"Yep," Ella said. "Saturday at Metr-APE-olis."

The scouts exchanged empty expressions. With the back of his hand, Richie wiped ketchup from his chin. Then the four of them rose from the booth and stepped outside. As they made their way to the front gates, no one said a word. To Noah, the silence felt strange. It was as if they all wanted to save their words for whatever they might face on Saturday—whatever they might discover in Metr-APE-olis. Noah had had enough experience in the Secret Zoo to know that could be just about anything.

CHAPTER 2

THE MYSTERY OF METR-APE-OLIS

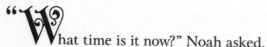

"What time is it now?" Noah asked.

Megan checked her watch. "Just past eight."

Noah scanned the cold zoo landscape a final time. It was barren. Except for his friends, he couldn't see a single person, and most of the animals were tucked away in caves and other warm spots. He stared up at the Metr-APE-olis building. It was enormous—four stories high and constructed from bricks the size of shoe boxes.

"Okay," said Noah. He waved the scouts forward, leading them up the brick path to the front door of the exhibit. Around them, crisp autumn leaves whirled.

A man's voice rang out behind them. "Hey! Hold up over there!"

The scouts spun around. Strolling toward them was a tall, lanky man. The wind swirled his shock of red hair, making it look like his head was on fire. Charlie Red, a Clarksville Zoo security guard . . . and their nemesis. Wagging his finger, he said, "The zoo ain't open! How did—" His words stopped and his eyebrows dropped when he realized who he was talking to. "Oh—*you*. What the heck are you doing here so early?"

Ella stepped forward, hands on her hips. "We're on special scout business—at the orders of Mr. Darby!"

Charlie Red threw back his head and howled with laughter. "Well, well! Special scout business! Now, that *does* sound important."

"Knock it off, Red," said Ella. "You need to deal with the fact that we're part of the team now."

"The team?" Charlie stepped up to Ella, lowered his head, and pushed his face close to hers. "You ain't part of no team, kid! You're a bunch of spoiled brats that snooped your way into something you got no business being part of. You might be on Mr. Darby's good side, but as soon as everyone sees what a mistake it is to keep you guys around, you'll be out of here. You're nothing but a bunch of—"

"Button it, Red!" Ella barked. She leaned forward, the

tip of her nose nearly touching Charlie's. "You think you scare us? If you don't stay out of our way, I'll have Tank drop-kick you over the zoo wall."

Charlie shot her a menacing look, then turned to leave. As he headed down the path, he called back to them, "I'll be watching the four of you runts. Believe me—I'll be watching!"

The scouts watched him go, then headed into Metr-APE-olis. The doors creaked and groaned, as if annoyed at being opened. As they slammed behind the scouts, their latches clicked sharply shut.

Metr-APE-olis was the size of a vast warehouse and contained a small jungle. The trees weren't real, but it was impossible to tell. Their trunks were thick—too thick for an ape to wrap its arms around—and the branches started low to the ground, just above the apes' heads. Streams wound across the grassy floor, and waterfalls plunged from the heights.

Visitors to Metr-APE-olis could explore the exhibit from within a maze of glass tunnels. Outside the clear walls, the exhibit was entirely open. Apes could walk up at any point along the passage and put themselves mere inches from the visitors.

Metr-APE-olis got its name partly from the small huts that were nestled in the trees, creating the feeling of an elevated city. Constructed mostly of bamboo, these huts were often connected to one another by rope bridges or monkey bars. Tire swings dangled from branches, and apes played in them, twirling and swinging and bouncing around.

As the scouts headed down one of the tunnels, Noah said, "Okay, I guess we find Daisy."

"Which one is she?" asked Ella.

"She's a gorilla—that's all I know. I'm hoping she'll recognize us."

The scouts followed the tunnel through several winding turns and soon found themselves near the middle of Metr-APE-olis. Here a gorilla pushed off its grassy seat and hoisted itself into the air. Then it dropped forward onto its knuckles, balancing on its hands and feet. Sniffing the air, the gorilla fixed its stare on the scouts, swaying softly from side to side.

In the tunnel, the scouts halted. Noah said, "That's got to be Daisy."

"Yeah . . ." Ella rapped her knuckles against the tunnel. "But what are we supposed to do about *this*?"

Noah looked up and down the glass. He realized that it consisted of small segments joined together by seams. He slowly walked down the tunnel, stroking his fingers along the wall.

"Knowing what we know about the Clarksville Zoo," he said, "how could we get to the other side of this glass?"

It was Richie who answered. "Maybe from outside the building?"

"I'm not so sure." Noah continued to slide his fingertips along the glass. When he had gone about thirty feet away from his friends, he stood still and concentrated his touch against one of the seams. "Hmmm . . ."

"What?" asked Megan. "What are you thinking?"

"I'm thinking about how creative our friends are." He reached over his head and ran his hand down the vertical seam. Then he pointed to a seam on his left, only a few feet away, and said, "Right here—this edge and that one. Don't you think they're pretty close?"

The scouts peered in both directions. All the other sections were more than twenty feet wide.

Noah reached his arms out and touched both seams at the same time. "When the Secret Society first built this tunnel, they made this piece really small."

The scouts gathered around him and felt the glass wall. Meanwhile, Daisy knuckle-walked toward them. She stopped about twenty feet away from the tunnel and faced the scouts, still on her hands and feet. Then she shook the tension out of her shoulders, tipped her head, and locked eyes with Noah. With a snort and a grunt, she leaned forward, bracing herself.

Noah dropped his arms and said, "Uhhh . . . guys? I think we better back up."

"Why?" said Richie.

Daisy lurched forward. On all fours, she charged the glass, her furred muscles shuddering.

"Move!" Noah shouted. He wrapped his arms around his friends and pushed them away from the wall. Richie tripped over his own flashy feet and fell in a heap.

Daisy dropped her shoulder forward and crashed into the tunnel, directly between the two close-together seams. The wall shook, knocking her backward. She regained her stance and walked back to her former spot, where she turned, pounded her chest, and dropped to her knuckles once more. She snorted and fixed her stare on the glass.

Richie jumped up and darted behind Ella. Peering over her shoulder, he said, "You don't mind, do you?"

"It won't be the first time you've used me as a human shield," said Ella.

Daisy dropped her head, charged, and rammed the tunnel again. This time the glass segment did more than just shake—this time it rose into the air, and tipped up and back, as if hinged to the ground behind them. It lifted two feet, three feet, and finally stopped four feet above the ground. Daisy stuck her head into the opening and roared, revealing the pink cavity of her mouth and the sharp points of her stained fangs. She struck her fists against her chest and cast a hard stare at the scouts.

"Uhhh . . ." Ella said, "you never really get used to this

kind of thing—gorillas opening secret passages and stuff."

"She's letting us in," said Noah. "C'mon—let's go."

He ducked his head and slipped through the open wall. The other scouts followed. As Richie passed Daisy, he brushed his shoulder against hers. The gorilla grunted and showed her teeth.

"Oops!" Richie squeaked. He raised his hands and swung his body away from her. "My bad, my bad."

Seconds after the scouts exited the tunnel, the elevated wall fell closed again, snapping into place along the seams. The scouts turned and watched Daisy. She strode up to them, sniffed the air, and batted her eyes.

"I guess . . . I guess you know who we are," said Megan. "Mr. Darby said you'd be able to help us."

Daisy didn't react.

Snapping each syllable out, Richie said, *"We—need—in—side—Se—cret—Zoo."*

The gorilla furrowed her brow. She tipped her head to one side and stared at Richie, as if trying to figure out what was wrong with him.

"Nice job, Richie," Ella commented. "It's good to have you along to bridge the language gap."

Daisy backed away from the scouts, stopping at a tree full of chimps. For a moment, she simply stared at the four friends, as if waiting for something. Then she hammered her fists against her chest, startling the scouts off their feet. She turned and walked off, her big rump swaying.

"Where's she going?" Megan asked.

"No idea," answered Noah. "But let's follow her."

Daisy led the scouts to a flat, grassy spot between two trees. Five tire swings dangled from the branches, their ropes disappearing into the dense foliage overhead.

Daisy knuckle-walked to one of the tires and gripped it in her mighty hands. Grunting, she gave the tire a shake. She stared straight at the scouts.

"Uh-oh," said Richie. "Anyone thinking what I'm thinking?"

"The tires—they're the way into the Secret Zoo," said Megan. "But . . . *how*?"

Walking to one of the swings, Noah said, "There's one way to find out." He coiled his fingers around the rope and slipped his legs inside the tire. Nothing happened, but Daisy jumped up and down excitedly.

"C'mon, guys," said Megan as she walked over to another swing. Ella followed. The girls stepped into two tires, seating their rear ends against the rubbery inner circles.

Richie didn't move.

"C'mon, Richie," Megan urged. "It can't be that bad."

"You know . . . I could always wait here. Maybe I could—"

"Richie!" Ella snapped.

"Okay, okay!"

Each of the scouts was now seated in a tire swing. Noah's and Megan's tires dangled from one tree, and Richie's and Ella's from the other. The tires swayed softly back and forth, making the overhead branches creak. The expanse of Metr-APE-olis suddenly felt empty and quiet—a place for echoes.

Ella said, "Ummm . . . in case you guys haven't noticed, nothing's happening."

"Maybe we need to swing," Noah suggested.

To get the tire rocking, Noah dropped his back and kicked his legs forward. As the swing began to move, Daisy dashed over and stopped it.

"Or," Noah added, "maybe not."

Noah realized that Daisy was staring at a rope bridge above them. He followed her gaze. A chimp ran across the wobbly planks, its shoulders seesawing, and jumped into the attached hut. Daisy let out what seemed to be a grunt of satisfaction.

From the hut came a screeching sound, like a lever being worked into place, and all at once the tire swings dropped a few inches. Noah peered overhead but couldn't see anything through the leaves.

Then he heard a second squeal—another lever had been thrown. Immediately, the ground dropped out from under the scouts' feet. Four square hatches had opened, one beneath each of them, like trapdoors. They gave way to dark caverns in the earth. Noah watched as small rocks soundlessly tumbled into the void beneath his feet.

Noah glanced at Richie. Wide-eyed and pale, his friend was staring into the empty hole beneath him. Just above the pit dangled Richie's fabulously bright running shoes.

"Guys . . ." said Noah.

The scouts answered in unison, "Yeah?"

"Don't . . . don't let go of the ropes."

At this piece of advice, a screech from the hut announced another lever being thrown, and all at once the four tires plunged into the holes. Around the scouts, the world went black and the air turned damp—cold and thick, with an earthy aroma.

The scouts were on their way into the Secret Zoo. Again.

✿ CHAPTER 3 ✿

INSIDE THE SECRET METR-APE-OLIS

Noah continued to fall—to fall and fall and fall. The air whirled around him, lifting the back of his jacket and whapping the earflaps of his cap against his head.

He lost all sense of time and could only guess how much had passed. Occasionally, the falling tire skipped off one of the walls, sending tremors through the rubber. Worried that his feet might get pinched, Noah wrapped his ankles together and straightened his legs directly beneath him.

Something soft and smooth brushed his body. In an instant, it was gone, but Noah knew what it had been:

velvet. A velvet curtain marking the entrance into the Secret Zoo.

The tire fell out of the darkness into a bright space filled with trees. Noah screamed, partly with fear and partly with relief at being released from the dark unknown of the cave. As the tire dropped through a thick web of branches, Noah saw that he was falling into a jungle—a jungle that was undoubtedly contained within the walls of a sector in the Secret Zoo. Huge trees filled the space, sunlight stabbing through their branches. Vines dangled in the air, some falling limply across branches and others looping back into the heights. More than five hundred feet below lay a grassy plain.

Noah craned his neck to look upward. The tire swing had punched through an opening in the bend of an enormous branch. Somehow, the ordinary exhibit in the Clarksville Zoo came to an end in the hollow of an extraordinary tree.

Across the trees stretched the winding trails of long parallel bars—monkey bars, like those in the Metr-APE-olis exhibit above. Nestled in the treetops were countless wooden huts. Some were elaborate, with roofs and open doors, and others were simple, nothing more than platforms wedged between the branches. Long-reaching rope bridges joined the huts to distant trees. Staircases spiraled down many of the trunks.

Noah spotted the other scouts, each falling at a different speed. At least a hundred feet below him was Ella, while Richie was more than a hundred feet above him. Thoughtless with panic, Richie was twirling his tire, sending it jerking in every direction, bumping branches and bursting through meshes of leaves. Halfway between Noah and Richie was Megan.

Finally, Noah realized with relief that his tire was slowing, and he relaxed his white-knuckled grip on the rope. He approached a distant platform set in the trees, a simple collection of wooden planks with no walls or rails. Oddly shaped with seven sides of different lengths and angles, the platform had been custom-built to fit the unique grip of the surrounding branches. It was the size of a small parking lot and covered with chimpanzees, as many as a hundred. They were rushing about, stomping, rolling, and leaping off one another's backs.

Ella was the first to land, touching down near the center of the platform. As she stepped out of her tire, she was immediately surrounded by chimps. The rambunctious apes shrieked and hollered and swatted their palms against the planks beneath their feet.

Noah touched down next and slipped out onto the wooden floor. Released from his weight, the tire sprang into the air, bouncing off the occasional branch as it headed back up to the Clarksville City Zoo.

Ella glanced at Noah and then returned her attention to the commotion around her, saying, "These stupid things won't leave me alone!"

Noah squeezed into the crowd and joined his friend. As the two of them fended off the half-crazed chimps, Megan touched down on the platform. Noah couldn't believe how calm his sister was. She had been through so much in the past few weeks. Could anyone but Megan have survived being trapped in a cave for weeks by dangerous animals in an underground fantasy world? Noah knew the fact that she was here now, back in the Secret Zoo with the other scouts, was a testament to her courage.

Megan stepped out and let the chimps sniff her fingers. Then she gently stroked their heads.

"Check out Megan," Noah said to Ella. "It's like she's been dealing with these things her entire life."

"Well," said Ella, batting away another chimp, "she does hang out with you and Richie."

Noah couldn't resist smiling. Hearing Richie's name made him wonder where his friend was. He looked up and spotted him twirling in his plunging tire, about sixty feet above their heads. When he finally came to a stop above the platform, he tumbled out and hit the planks with a thump, a thud, and an *"Oomph!"*

"Nice entrance, Richie," said Ella. She boxed another chimp away. "Thanks for proving again that dodos can fly."

As the rope drew Richie's tire back into the heights of the Secret Metr-APE-olis, he peered up at his friends, his eyeglasses cocked to one side and a dazed look on his face. "Am I okay? Did I break anything?"

Ella said, "Maybe the world record for the longest distance ever traveled by a nerd with his butt in a tire—but if you mean bones, nope, I don't think so."

Richie patted his arms, his legs, his ribs. "Are you sure I'm not injured? Because I feel like I *should* be injured."

Ella pushed through the crowd and grabbed Richie by his jacket collar, hoisting him to his feet. "Quit worrying!"

The chimps bounced over to Richie and studied him, curious, their hairless eyebrows raised. They rocked back and forth, bumping into one another and grunting. One poked Richie in his belly button, and he swatted its furry hand.

Noah worked his way through the crowd to stand at an edge of the platform and stare out at the sector, one of the many that joined a Clarksville Zoo exhibit to the City of Species, the core of the Secret Zoo. He stretched out his legs, lay flat on his stomach, and peered directly beneath the platform. The scouts were about five hundred feet off the ground, and there was no direct way off—no ladder, no rope bridge, no staircase. The only way down would be to climb to a nearby tree and descend from there.

Noah stood and gazed across the Secret Metr-APE-olis, trying to locate the end of the sector—the entrance into the City of Species. These entrances were normally marked. It took some searching, but he found it. On a platform about two hundred yards away hung a velvet curtain beneath a blinking light.

"Over there!" Noah called out as he pointed at the curtain. "The entrance to the City of Species!" As his friends joined him, he said, "The only way we're going to get off this thing is to climb to another tree."

"Whoa!" said Richie, holding up his palms and stepping backward. "I'm not so good in the trees!"

"Then we go to Plan B," Megan said.

The scouts stared at her, puzzled.

Ella said, "And that would be . . . ?"

"C'mon, you guys," Megan groaned. "The three of you know this place better than I do!"

She leaned forward and whispered something in a chimp's ear. The chimp raised its eyebrows, pursed its lips, and grunted. Then it ran to the edge of the platform, jumped into the trees, and swung swiftly through the branches, calling out to the other apes in its strange language.

Richie looked confused. "Megan—what did you say?"

Megan shrugged her shoulders. "I just asked for some help."

"Wonderful," Richie said. "Why do I have a feeling I'm not going to like this?"

Not far from the platform with the velvet curtain, the chimp climbed into the treetops and disappeared. The scouts stood by, watching in silence.

Across the long reach of the sector, the treetops began to quake as hundreds of apes descended. Chimps and orangutans scurried down trunks and heaved across branches until they had aligned themselves in a perfect single file between the two platforms—the one on which the scouts stood and the distant one with the velvet curtain. They held on to anything and everything: branches, monkey bars, vines, staircases, huts, and trees. No two apes were more than fifteen feet apart. The first orangutan in front of the scouts clung to a tree, its eyes fixed on the four friends, its arm reaching toward them.

"You guys see what's going on, right?" Megan asked. When no one responded, she added, "You remember connect-the-dots? Just think of the apes as the dots and us as the ink."

The color drained from Richie's face as he realized what Megan was getting at. "I think I hate you now."

Megan's smile broke into laughter. "C'mon, Richie," she said. "This is going to rock!"

CHAPTER 4

THE SWING OF THINGS

"Maybe I'm not the brightest bulb on the Christmas tree," Ella said. "But *connect-the-dots*? What are you talking about?"

Megan walked back through the chimps, briefly touching her palms to their heads as she moved past. About thirty feet in from the edge of the platform, she turned and faced not only her friends, but the first orangutan in the line of apes across the trees.

Noah understood what his sister was thinking. "Megan, you sure about this?" he asked.

"No," Megan said. "But we trust Mr. Darby, right? I don't

think he'd put us in danger, not without warning us first."

With that, she ran through the crowd, past the scouts, and threw herself over the edge of the platform.

The orangutan shot out its long arm, seized Megan's wrist, and swung her forward. At the farthest point of its reach, it sprang open its fingers, releasing her. Megan soared to the next ape in line, a chimpanzee who was already reaching behind itself with an open hand. The oafish-looking chimp cinched Megan's wrist and pitched her around, just as the ape before it had done.

The catch-and-throw of the first two apes had been easy enough, but Megan knew what would make it easier. She could swing across the animals, treating their hands like monkey bars. She just needed to twist her body, alternate her arms, and heave her weight. In the air between the second and third ape, Megan dropped one arm and reached the other forward, pivoting at the same time. When the third chimp seized her wrist, she grabbed the chimp's, and together they swung her weight forward, their arms locked like two acrobats on a trapeze. When the chimp let go, she soared forward, an arm and a leg extended in both directions.

Glancing at Ella and Richie, Noah said, "You see what she's doing, right?"

"Yep," said Ella. She elbowed a chimp that had stepped on her toes and added, "I'm just afraid she's making it look easy."

"We can do this," Noah said. "It's not like we haven't done this kind of thing a million times. How often have we swung across the branches in Fort Scout?"

With that, Noah took ten steps back and then dashed to the edge of the platform. Screaming, he lunged into the air, his right arm pushed forward, ready to lock grasps with the first ape.

"I'm next," said Ella. She brushed past Richie and walked several apes deep into the crowd. "There's only one way across this place, so I better cowgirl up." She charged forward, her ponytail whipping across her shoulders. Then she sailed toward the orangutan's outstretched arm.

Richie stepped cautiously to the edge of the platform. The orangutan in the tree stared at him. It tipped its head to one side, then the other, then grunted. It slammed a fist against its chest, opened its hands toward Richie, and rolled its fingertips on and off its palms, beckoning him.

Richie glanced over his shoulders. "Me?" He inched forward and stopped. With his fingers cupped around his mouth, he called out, "You sure you got enough strength left?"

The orangutan threw back its head and roared, exposing its crooked yellow teeth. Then, still reaching for Richie, it shook the limb it was hanging from, whipping the leafy twigs through the air.

"Okay, okay . . ." Richie thought about it for a few seconds before he backed up at least twenty feet. "Here goes."

He broke into a run. At the end of the platform, he halted so suddenly that his glasses slipped to the tip of his nose and nearly fell off his face. With his toes pointed over the edge, he stared into the green abyss, his heart racing. The faraway plain was peppered with gorillas.

A loud screech dazed his senses. He felt a tug at his jacket collar and glanced backward to find himself nose to nose with a chimp, whose cavernous mouth released a foul fog all over his glasses.

"He-help!" Richie sputtered.

Richie's legs shot up behind him and his head dropped forward as he was suspended above the platform in the grasp of the chimpanzee. His arms dangled beneath his body.

His world began to swing back and forth—the ape was rocking him, preparing to throw him toward the orangutan in the tree.

"Uh . . . nice chimp!" Richie stammered. "Um . . . good chimp! Chimp no throw Richie over edge! Chimp no—"

His words broke into an open scream as the ape hurled him forward.

Up and outward he went, as if in slow motion. His vision grazed the faraway grass dotted with gorillas. Then he saw the orangutan arm stretched out to grab him. Richie reached forward and focused on the ape's hand, which grew larger and larger until he could clearly see its fingers: long, hairy, thick, and powerful enough to crush bones. The ape's hand was within inches of his own when something terrible happened. Richie stopped.

For an instant, he hung in the air, motionless. Then he plummeted.

As the world spun and whirled in front of him, something as coarse as sandpaper squeezed his wrist. Richie's body jolted and his stomach dropped. The orangutan had leaped down and snagged him out of the air. Richie tried to holler his gratitude, but discovered he was too terrified to shape a single intelligible word. What came out instead was a strange guttural roar, not unlike one of the many ape sounds: *"Geeaarrhhh-ahhh!"*

The orangutan pulled down its eyebrows at Richie. Then it hoisted him behind its body, winding up to pitch him back into the trees.

Richie tried to scream *"No!"* but instead produced another half-ape sound: *"Grrraahhhh!"*

The orangutan heaved its hairy arm around with a sweeping motion, like a bowler throwing a bowling ball. Then he released Richie, hurling him to the next ape.

"Nneeeeeaaah!" Richie screamed.

As he flew between the branches, he somehow managed to twist himself upside down, so the waiting chimp was forced to curl forward and grab his ankle. The ape swung around and pitched Richie into the air. Still upended, Richie had a headfirst view of the ground far below, which inspired him to utter real words instead of another meaningless sound: "Stop, you crazy apes!"

But the apes didn't stop, and Richie was airborne again. Still wrong side up, he sailed over a rope bridge covered with chimps. Excited by the sight of a flying boy, the apes jumped about and stomped their feet, rolling the planks in waves. As Richie's ankle was grabbed again, his passing stare happened upon a chimp that was twirling a pair of tied-together shoes above its head. Richie had enough sense left to find this at first odd, and then wildly incredible. Because not only was the chimp holding shoes, it was holding *Richie's* running shoes—the pair a gorilla had swiped off his feet when the scouts had first discovered the City of Species.

"My shoes!" Richie spluttered.

As he felt himself being let go again, he gave up trying to understand and turned to the crucial task at hand: not falling to his death. He continued to pass in and out of the hands of chimps and orangutans, twisting into strange new positions as he went. The apes were forced to grab his wrists, elbows, legs, and ankles. He crossed the sector at the same speed as the other scouts, but with far less grace. Ella might have called it "Richie style."

❧ CHAPTER 5 ❧

FOUR MYSTERIOUS ESCORTS

Megan was the first to touch down. She did so with ease, landing on her hands and knees and rolling once. As she jumped to her feet, the surrounding chimps, orangutans, and gibbons lurched out of her way. Seconds later, Noah hit the platform and tumbled to a stop, frightening the nearby primates off their feet. Next came Ella, who landed upright and elected to run out her momentum rather than drop into a roll. The three scouts huddled near the center of the platform.

"Wow!" said Ella as she fixed her crooked earmuffs. "You can't do *that* on the playground. Anyone lose breakfast?"

Megan beamed. "That totally, totally rocked!"

Pointing into the trees, Noah said, "Look, guys—there's Richie!"

Richie was less than five apes from landing on the new platform. His body flailed in the air, looking boneless and limp. He soared backward, his rear end aimed at the ceiling. The chimp who'd tossed him had had to bury its fingers in the waistband of Richie's pants before heaving him along.

Ella shook her head. "Only Richie."

The three scouts broke into a fit of laughter, and the surrounding apes came alive with excitement. Near Megan, a white gibbon leaped onto the shoulders of a gorilla and pushed off backward, doing a complete flip.

Richie flew in headfirst, hitting the wooden planks with a crash. His body rolled and spun, taking out the legs of gibbons and chimps before finally stopping at the feet of the scouts.

Richie staggered to his feet and faced the others. His glasses were cocked sideways, and his cap looked ready to fall off. As pale as a snowman, he belched into his fist, then said, "That wasn't so bad."

Noah wasn't sure whether he was trying to convince himself or his friends.

Her voice soft with unusual tenderness, Ella said, "You did it, Richie!" Then she reached up, straightened his glasses, and became her normal self again: "Now put your pieces back together so we can find Mr. Darby."

Richie fixed his cap. Then, with a pinch and a pull, he loosened the uncomfortable wedgie that an orangutan had given him. Together, the scouts turned and headed toward the velvet curtain. As they made their way, the apes jumped to either side, opening a path. Sitting in the trees, perched atop the huts, and straddling the monkey bars, all the apes in the sector had their attention fixed on the scouts.

When they were only a few steps from the curtain, four bodies dropped out of the trees and landed in front of them with a quick succession of thumps, scattering apes. They were human, the first people the scouts had seen in the Secret Metr-APE-olis. Their landings left them crouched in front of the scouts, their faces turned downward.

All across the forest, the apes fell silent.

One by one, the newcomers rose and raised their stares. They were teenagers, not much older than the scouts. And like the scouts, two of them were girls and two were boys.

Noah and his friends said nothing, using their silence to communicate a message: they were not going to be the ones to speak first. That responsibility lay with the teenagers in front of them—the ones who had just blocked their passage into the City of Species.

The boy standing directly in front of Noah had shocking green eyes, partly hidden behind strands of sloppy brown hair, which fell across his shoulders. He wore a brown leather jacket with vertical pleats on the front and back, and faded blue jeans that were shredded at the knees, exposing terrible scars that ran in all directions. His jacket was covered with zippers and gleaming steel buckles.

Noah's eyes shifted to the other boy. A scraggly beard dangled on his chin. A tight knit cap with a two-inch brim covered his forehead and the tips of his ears. It was pulled down so low in front that the boy had to tip his head back to see. His piercing, bright eyes contrasted with his ebony skin. He had broad, powerful shoulders and wore a pleated jacket, but his was black and had fewer buckles. His fingerless gloves had thick velcro straps. But what really caught Noah's attention was the enormous canvas backpack on his shoulders. With wide, bulging pockets and numerous zippers, it had a military feel.

Noah looked at one of the girls. She was beautiful. Her hair and her skin had a rich sheen. She had soft, knowing eyes and smooth hair that looped her ears and spilled down her back. Like the boys, she wore a jacket, but hers was soft blue with pinholes all over it, and like the boy with the backpack, she wore fingerless gloves.

The other girl was pretty, but in a hardened way. She had olive skin and blond hair cut to different lengths: the back was clipped short; the top stood out in all directions; and her bangs, dyed red, fell messily across her forehead. Her clothes were entirely different from those of her companions. A sleeveless T-shirt clung to her body, and she didn't wear a jacket. Purple leather boots stopped just short of her knees. Their thick soles reminded Noah of the platform boots he'd seen in old pictures—the kind that seemed possible to stomp out a campfire with. The girl continually chomped a wad of gum, blowing and bursting tiny bubbles.

Each teenager had thin velvet strips stitched to different spots on their clothes. Uniquely shaped, they looked like accents. The ones with jackets had them on their collars, wrists, and shoulders. The ones with gloves had them on the backs of their hands. The girl with wild hair had squiggly strips on her boots.

After a long, awkward silence, the boy with the long hair spoke. "Darby told us to meet you. Told us you'd need some help."

Hearing Mr. Darby referred to as "Darby" seemed strange and disrespectful. Noah didn't like it.

"Put your arms down and relax already," the boy added. "It's not like we're here to bust you up."

Noah realized he was still guarding the scouts with

his arms. "How do we know that?"

"Because you're not already busted up." The kid lifted his chin toward Noah, a sort of greeting. "I'm Sam. You got a name?"

Noah slowly lowered his arms and paused before answering. "Noah."

Sam swept back his long bangs. "This your crew?"

Noah pointed to his friends, stating their names: "Megan, my sister. Ella. And Richie."

Sam jerked his thumb in the direction of his companions. "My friends," he said. He put his hand on the other boy's shoulder. "Tameron." Pointing to the attractive girl, he said, "Over there's Solana, and"—he motioned to the girl with the wild hair—"that's Hannah."

Feeling awkward and not knowing why, Noah waved.

"Now that everyone knows everyone," Sam said, "let's do this."

"What, exactly, is *this*?" Richie asked.

"Darby wants us to take you to the Library of the Secret Society." Sam started to walk off, stopped, then turned back to the scouts. "Look, let me get something out into the open. We're not here to be your buds, and we're sure not too thrilled with this *thing* Darby's given us."

"What thing?" Noah said. "What are you talking about—walking us to the City of Species?"

Tameron spoke up. He, too, seemed irritated. "Darby

wants us to babysit you for the next year—like we don't have anything better to do."

Sam and Solana nodded in agreement. Hannah popped her gum.

"What are you—" Noah's confusion pulled his thoughts up short. "The next year? Who said anything about the next year?"

The apes on the platform watched the scene develop, nervously glancing over one another's shoulders. In the trees, apes stared down over vines and limbs and bridges.

"Didn't Darby tell you?" Solana asked.

Noah was about to say something when Ella stepped in front of him. All he could see of her was the back of her head—the bouncing ponytail and the pink globes of her furry earmuffs.

"The only thing Mr. Darby's told us is that someone was going to meet us here," Ella said. "What's wrong with you guys? Why are you treating us like we've done something wrong?"

Tameron grunted. "Like you haven't?"

"What are you *talking* about?" Ella shot back.

Tameron said, "We have sasquatches on the loose because of you."

Noah saw Megan look away in shame. If she had never made her way into the Secret Zoo, forcing a rescue by the Secret Society, the sasquatches never would have escaped into the City of Species from their barricaded sector. Megan had once told the scouts that she felt responsible for all the trouble they caused.

"Whatever!" Ella said. "Maybe if you guys knew how to protect your borders, we wouldn't have this problem right now! We did what it took to break Megan out! And we did it without the help of *some* people around here!" Ella glared at each of the teenagers. "It seems this place has its share of wimps!"

"*What?*" Sam snapped.

"Where were you when we went into the Dark Lands to rescue Megan? Huh?"

"We were there," Solana said.

"How come I never saw—"

Noah grabbed Ella's elbow and pulled her back. "Everyone—knock it off! Mr. Darby asked us to come here, and Mr. Darby asked the four of you to meet us here. Let's not forget that he's the one in charge of this place."

Sam used his fingers to comb his bangs out of his eyes, saying, "Yep. And Darby gets what Darby wants. Nothing's ever changed about that."

Noah was confused by this confrontation. The teenagers were all troubled by something the scouts were not going to find out about by standing on this platform, trading stares and insults.

"C'mon, *Action Scouts*," Sam said, drawing out their name to mock it. "Follow us. And try not to step on too many tails."

He turned away from the group, pulled back the velvet curtain, and led his companions over the threshold. The colorful curtain swayed behind them, its tassels dancing on the wooden planks.

"Geez," said Richie. "Not the happiest bunch in the lot."

"No," said Noah. "Not at all."

"Forget about them," Ella blurted as she stepped toward the curtain. "We're here to talk to Mr. Darby, not to make friends." Then she slipped through the magical exit.

"I'm not so sure about that," Noah muttered as he reached for the curtain.

"What's that supposed to mean?" Megan asked.

To avoid having to reply, Noah stepped into the City of Species, the heart of the Secret Zoo.

ᵒᖇ CHAPTER 6 ᖇᵒ

OLD FRIENDS, FAMILIAR CITY

Noah stood beside Ella, and together they stared out at the City of Species. Though the scouts had been there only a couple weeks ago, seeing it now was like seeing it for the first time.

The City of Species was part city, part forest. Each part seemed to need the other, and their bizarre marriage was breathtaking. Tall buildings were surrounded by trees whose limbs reached through their walls, splitting steel and piercing glass. Waterfalls fell from rooftops, splashing across balconies and limbs before spilling into fountains and streams, bursting into mist. Streetlights blinked beneath low-hanging branches, and ivy pinned signs to the sides of brick buildings. All types of animals passed down the winding streets. They crawled through intersections, slithered along sidewalks, hopped over hedges, and swept across the sky.

To Noah's right, a section of the street the size of a football field was missing. In its place was a body of water. Waves rolled across its surface and lapped the concrete shoreline. Powerful stone buildings dove into the depths. Through the lens of the water, the submerged floors appeared to sway. Clinging to the stone-faced buildings were crabs, lobsters, starfish, and barnacles of all shapes and sizes. Schools of exotic fish were swimming about— shimmering flashes of color—as were sharks, dolphins, seals, and turtles. Noah saw several humans swim by in green diving suits.

At the street level, a narrow road crossed the water. Made of wood, it floated like a long dock. Elephants, giraffes, and countless smaller animals traversed it. The floating road supported their weight so easily that ripples barely formed in the water.

"Awesome," Noah muttered.

A complicated mesh of tree limbs grew overhead. The leaves had turned color since the last time the scouts were here, autumn having reached the City of Species later than in the outside world. Leaves rained down, momentarily tattooing the backs of larger animals, and birds flew among the falling color.

"How come the leaves are turning just now?" Noah asked.

"Don't know," Ella said. "Guess the seasons are different in the City of Species."

"And the time," Noah said. "When we were here last, the time was way off. We came in at night, and here it was day."

Ella shrugged. "Questions for Mr. Darby, I guess."

Noah felt something bump against his back. He spun around to find Richie, numb with awe, gazing at everything around them.

"What do you think?" asked Noah. "More awesome than last time, huh?"

Richie said, "This place—it's just unreal."

Megan emerged through the curtain and joined her friends on the sidewalk. She stared in wonder at the city.

The scouts heard a voice. "You guys coming, or what?" They turned and saw Sam standing before them, his hands planted firmly on his hips.

"C'mon!" he barked. "Darby's waiting for us!"

Sam's impatience made Noah realize that somehow people could actually grow used to the City of Species. It was even possible to take it for granted.

Noah nodded to his friends and said, "Let's go."

The scouts joined the teenagers, and together, the eight of them started toward the Library of the Secret Society. Not long into their journey, they came upon an elaborate marble building. On each side, lines of columns supported a series of small arched rooftops. Winding staircases led to high balconies beneath vaulted ceilings. On every balcony, a velvet curtain hung. The building's white facade was covered with stained-glass windows, and high up, the building disappeared into the colorful treetops.

"Wow!" Noah said. "Check this place out!"

For a closer look, he stepped onto a stairway that led to the main entrance, only to be snagged and pulled back by Sam.

"Nuh-uh," Sam pointed to the top of the stairway. "Read the flag."

Noah gazed above the landing and saw a red flag hanging from a vaulted ceiling. Rippling in the breeze, the flag read, THE SECTOR OF DESCENT, and beneath that, SECTOR FOUR OF THE FORBIDDEN FIVE.

"Forbidden Five?" Noah asked as he allowed Sam to lead him up the street, pulling his arm. "What's that supposed to mean?"

"Just what it says—it's forbidden." Sam shot Noah a serious look. "There are five sectors that are off-limits to everyone but a select few in the Secret Society, and you guys are not part of that select few."

Noah deliberated for a moment and replied with a question. "What are the other sectors?"

Sam was quiet, as if he might not answer. Finally, he did. "The Dark Lands, Creepy Critters, the Cemetery Sector, and . . ."—Sam's voice trailed off and then returned—"and one more."

"One more?" Noah said. "What's it called?"

"Don't worry about it right now," said Sam.

Noah pulled away and rejoined his friends, whispering, "Do these guys need a lesson in manners, or what?" As they continued up the street, he glanced over his shoulder and read the flag once more: THE SECTOR OF DESCENT— SECTOR FOUR OF THE FORBIDDEN FIVE. What did it mean? And why was it forbidden?

Suddenly, they saw a group of animals charging toward them. One was a polar bear, another was a penguin, the third was a rhinoceros, and racing at their feet was a small coterie of prairie dogs. These were not ordinary animals—at least not to the scouts. They were Blizzard, Podgy, Little Bighorn, and P-Dog and his companions, and they had closely shared the scouts' first adventure in the Secret Zoo.

The four of them rushed toward the animals, cheering. Noah wrapped his arms around Blizzard's long neck, and the mighty polar bear softly growled and nudged his wide, wet snout against the boy's shoulder, dotting his jacket.

"Bliz!" said Noah. "It feels like I haven't seen you in months!"

Podgy squeezed his way in front of Blizzard. Nearly four feet tall, the emperor penguin was almost the same height as Noah. "Podge!" Noah said. "You've been practicing your flying, right?"

Podgy, who'd only recently learned to fly, confirmed by wagging his long flippers.

Megan walked up to Podgy and put her hand on his head. "Remember me, bud?"

The big penguin waddled from side to side with excitement. He had helped rescue Megan from a cave in the Dark Lands.

Little Bighorn plodded over to Ella and Richie, who wrapped their arms over the rhino's leathery neck. Little Bighorn rolled his head, whacking Richie affectionately with the side of his horn.

"Ow!" Richie teased. He straightened his glasses and said, "Gentle with the specs!"

Little Bighorn snorted and lifted his massive head, raising Ella and Richie a few feet off the street.

"Whoa!" Ella said. "Don't put me back in the trees—I just got out of them!"

Seven prairie dogs scampered up to Richie. P-Dog stood on his hind legs, yipped twice, and twitched his nose.

Richie dropped to one knee and scratched the chubby

prairie dog's head. "What's up, P-Dog? I bet you didn't expect to see us back so soon, huh?"

The other prairie dogs surrounded Richie, sniffing his feet and investigating the glare of his running shoes—the same glare they'd been so curious about the last time Richie had been here.

"Pretty cool, huh?" Richie stuck one foot forward, adding, "Check it out—new shoes."

He suddenly stood straight and faced the other scouts. "When we were crossing the Metr-APE-olis sector, did you guys see that chimp with my old shoes?"

"Huh?" said Noah.

"My shoes. Some chimp had them. You didn't see that?"

"Nuh-uh."

Ella said, "But of course, we didn't spend most of our time upside down like you."

"Well, I saw them. And if they're still out there, I'm getting them back."

Ella asked, "Do you really care about a stinky old pair of shoes?"

"It's a principle thing."

Ella rolled her eyes and the scouts returned their attention to their animal friends.

Megan said to Tameron, "These animals—we met them last time we were here."

Tameron tipped his head back and stared down on

Megan. "Like we don't know that, kid." He turned to walk off, saying, "C'mon—we got to jet."

Solana threw her shiny hair off her shoulders and looked at the scouts and the animals. "It's great you guys are so in love with one another, but we've got a job to do."

Blizzard swung his snout in Solana's direction and snarled.

Casually, she said, "Knock it off, Bliz. You know we don't have time to waste."

"Wait a minute," Noah said, glancing between Solana and Blizzard. "You two . . . you know each other?"

Solana nodded. Beside her, Hannah blew a small bubble that quickly burst against her lips.

"But with so many animals, how—?"

"Blizzard, Podgy, Little Big, P—we know all the big players around here," said Solana.

Noah wasn't sure he liked the teenagers knowing their animal friends. The escorts had been treating the scouts so rudely that Noah preferred to keep them at a distance.

"C'mon!" Sam said. "Let's speed it up already!"

He led his friends down the street into the crowd of busy animals. Noah and Megan clambered onto Blizzard's back as Ella and Richie climbed onto Little Bighorn.

From the trees, a tiny bird swooped down. He had metallic blue wings, bright red legs, and an orange bill that was nearly as long as his body. He landed on Noah's shoulder and sidestepped until he found a spot that suited him.

"Marlo!" said Noah.

The kingfisher tipped his head from side to side and chirped loudly as he ruffled his feathers. Then he turned and pointed his long beak at Blizzard's second passenger.

Smiling, Megan said, "I'm along for the ride this time, Marlo."

Marlo chirped a second time and looked away.

Blizzard and Little Bighorn headed across the City of Species, the scouts shifting atop the animals' massive muscles. They wove through the crowded streets and caught up to the teenagers. Noah found himself beside Sam, who was talking to Tameron, his arm raised as he pointed to a building. Noah saw a zipper running along the seam of his sleeve and down his side to his waist. At the wrist, the metal slider had a C-shaped steel clip attached to it; near the waist, there was a steel buckle. Noah thought the slider and the buckle could clip together, allowing Sam to open the zipper just by raising his arm. But why would a jacket unzip in such a peculiar way?

Noah turned his attention back to the City of Species—its animals, its commotion, its magnificence. He studied the velvet curtains they passed. No two were the same. They had different colors, different textures, different sheens, and different tassels. He wondered why the curtains were necessary, and why they were made of velvet. They had a critical function in the Secret Zoo, but he didn't know how they worked. He wished he could ask one of the teenagers, but he knew what kind of answer he'd receive—in essence, "Shut up."

For now, Noah dismissed these concerns. He was looking forward to hearing what Mr. Darby had to say. He was also curious about the Library of the Secret Society. He couldn't imagine what it would be like, but he was certain it would be nothing less than spectacular.

CHAPTER 7

THE LIBRARY OF THE SECRET SOCIETY

The teenagers veered off the street and led the scouts between two columns with a blue banner that read, "The Library of the Secret Society" with shiny gold letters. They climbed a wide stairway that led to a massive, octagonal building with a high glass roof. The stairway surrounded the entire library, its sharp bends creating eight distinct sections. The top of each section had a landing with its own entrance into the building, and on each landing was a fountain from which water sprayed. Blizzard and Little Bighorn lumbered up the steps, their muscular backs shifting and pitching the scouts about.

The stairs were crowded with people and animals, all holding books. The animals had found unique ways to carry them. A kangaroo hopped past Noah, its pouch brimming with comics. A cheetah ran around Blizzard, its jaws locked on a thick dictionary. A komodo dragon slipped beneath Little Bighorn, books strapped to its back. Undoubtedly these animals were returning books on behalf of people. As intelligent as many of the Secret Zoo animals were, Noah was certain they couldn't read.

He stared up at the library, awestruck. At least twenty stories high, it was made of marble. On each story, a balcony stretched around the entire building. Trees grew on both sides of the library walls, their limbs reaching through the windows and marble blocks in both directions.

Noah wondered if P-Dog and Podgy would be able to climb the long staircase. He looked down and spotted the prairie dogs leaping from step to step, yipping in defiance of the challenge. Then Podgy flew past, his stomach a mound of blubber dangling beneath his flapping flippers. The penguin gracefully touched down at the top of the staircase beneath sprays of water that arched between two fountains.

"Nice landing, Podge!" Noah said.

Podgy pumped his flippers once to say thanks.

Blizzard heaved his weight over the top step engraved

with the words *Library of the Secret Society—Check it out!* The scouts and the animals followed their escorts to the closest entrance—a wide doorway draped with long trails of pearls and glass beads. People and animals flooded in and out through the doorway, making the beads clink together and reflect light in all directions. Once inside, Noah turned to watch the others. As P-Dog stepped in, he caught a bead in his eye and chomped at the offending glass globule. The others made it through without a problem.

"Holy smokes!" Richie gasped, craning his neck back and forth. "Look at this place!"

Noah was already doing just that. It would have been impossible not to. He guessed that it reached at least six hundred feet across, roughly the length of two football fields. Twenty stories above was an elaborate glass ceiling with painted engravings depicting the mingling of nature, animals, and books. Sunlight burst through it, streaking bright rays in which thousands of particles danced. Falling leaves colored the air, and fallen leaves carpeted the floor.

Trees and towering bookcases loomed over everything like walls in a colossal maze. The trees provided a framework for the bookcases. Shelves were attached to trunks, and rows of books were stacked along horizontal branches.

Along the inner perimeter of the library, Noah saw the same marble balconies that he'd seen on the outside. One per story, they shared the huge space with the trees and bookcases. Narrow walkways extended from them and stretched across the library to new places. People strolled along, skimming titles with their fingers and plucking books from the shelves.

Staring at the surroundings, Ella said, "You have got to be kidding." She made each word pop as she said it.

Noah said, "But the trees—they have to grow. What . . . what happens then?"

Solana surprised Noah by answering. "They adjust."

"Huh?"

"The bookcases—they adjust."

"Adjust? How?"

Solana answered by pointing up to a velvet patch near the spot where a tree limb had grown through a bookcase. Noah scanned the other bookcases. Wherever the trees had grown through the wood, similar velvet patches were nearby. He had seen these patches before—on the teenagers' clothes.

Noah's eyes dropped to the back of Solana's jacket, where strips of white velvet ran along the vertical seams. It was surely the same velvet that hung throughout the City of Species at the entrances to the sectors. *They adjust,* she had said. What exactly did that mean? And would Solana's jacket "adjust" because of its velvet?

Noah watched Sam lean over and whisper in Solana's ear. She nodded but said nothing.

"How does the velvet work?" Noah asked. "What gives the velvet its power?"

This time, Solana offered no response. Noah was sure she'd taken instructions from Sam to stop answering questions. It was becoming clear that the scouts couldn't trust the teenagers.

Noah frowned and returned his attention to the library. Monkeys crowded the heights. They wore blue vests that buttoned up in front, marking them as the first clothed animals that Noah had seen in the Secret Zoo. One of them would occasionally snatch a book from a shelf, climb to a bridge or jump to the ground, and pass it to a human patron.

"The monkeys . . ." Noah said to Megan. "They're handling books for people. They work here."

Megan nodded. "Too cool, huh?"

The group reached an intersection in the aisles, where they stopped to let a line of slow-moving sloths pass. Tameron propped his fists against his hips, irritated by the delay.

An old lady with beaded eyeglasses, plump cheeks, and a kind face came toward them. Deep wrinkles folded from the corners of her eyes. On her name tag was printed

"Mrs. Fellerton." She was walking beside a tortoise with a large wire box full of neatly stacked books strapped to its shell. The tortoise seemed to be acting as Mrs. Fellerton's book cart. She stopped directly beside Ella and Richie and said, "First time inside?"

"Yeah," said Ella. "But how . . . I mean . . . the books are so high. And the trees . . ."

Mrs. Fellerton chuckled. "We fetch most of the books for our patrons. It's always been that way. It must seem odd for someone who's visiting our library for the first time."

Noah saw the opportunity to get an answer to his question. He glanced at Sam to be sure he wasn't paying attention and leaned toward the librarian. "The velvet patches on the bookshelves—how do they get their power?"

The librarian smiled. "The power doesn't come from the velvet. The power comes from the books and the wisdom and worlds they contain." The kind lady swept her arm high in the air. "The velvet simply gathers the power in the books and materializes it into something you can see—which are the changes to the bookshelves."

Noah scrunched up his face. The librarian was talking in riddles.

"Be patient," said Mrs. Fellerton. "Knowledge comes with time. Nothing else."

"But . . ." Noah's voice trailed off when he realized the

librarian wasn't going to answer him directly.

Tameron turned to Little Bighorn and Blizzard and said, "C'mon, guys. Darby's this way."

The group hung a left turn and headed down an aisle so narrow that Little Bighorn's sides nearly rubbed against the shelves. Noah craned his neck. The towering wood-work made the space above him appear to narrow gradu-ally, an illusion created by the height of the bookcases.

The animals followed Tameron as he turned down another aisle, and another, and another. Nearing the middle of the library, the group heard the lulling splash of falling water.

"What's that noise?" Ella asked no one in particular.

"The Fountain Forum," Solana answered. "That's where we're headed."

Marlo turned on Noah's shoulder, brushing his feathers across the scout's cheek. Noah was reminded of another bird—Podgy. He peered over his shoulder to see the big penguin waddling along, staring blankly at his sur-roundings. Around him, the prairie dogs were chasing one another, racing between the books on the bottom shelves and tunneling in and out of the leaves. Podgy barely seemed to notice them—he just waddled forward, his flippers pressed flat against his sides and his webbed feet slinging colorful leaves into the air.

They rounded one more bookcase and stepped into

a clearing. Here, a circular formation of pillars pushed through the treetops and stretched hundreds of feet to the ceiling, where they helped support the glass roof. In the middle of the pillars was a long, oval fountain. Around it, people read books in plush chairs with wide armrests and pillowy ottomans. They looked utterly relaxed, as if on the verge of deep meditation or, perhaps, of falling asleep in the literal blink of their eyes.

As the scouts and their escorts passed the readers, an old man bounced out of a chair and dropped his book to his seat as his purple velvet trench coat draped around his feet. Narrow, rectangular sunglasses concealed his eyes but exposed his bushy eyebrows. His gray beard was as long and shaggy as his ponytail. Mr. Darby.

"Dear scouts!" he said. The old man brushed his hand down his beard. "I hope your travels weren't too arduous."

"I guess that depends on what *arduous* means," said Ella. "If it means being tossed through a jungle by a bunch of monkeys, then . . . yep . . . pretty arduous."

Mr. Darby smiled. "Once you learn to fully trust the apes, the Secret Metr-APE-olis will be a pleasure to cross."

From the chair beside Mr. Darby's, another man rose. The sheen on his bald head matched that of the shiny marble fountain. Towering over everyone, his body bulged with mounds of muscle. Tank.

"What's up, little dudes?" he said. "Welcome back."

Tank stepped forward and greeted Sam and the other teenagers. Instead of shaking their hands, he reached out his fist and, one by one, let the four of them softly punch it.

Megan leaned toward Noah and whispered, "You've got to be kidding me. Tank *likes* these jerks?"

Noah shrugged his shoulders. He was too confused to speak. Something was going on with the teenagers. Something peculiar.

Mr. Darby swung his arm toward the scouts' escorts, saying, "I see you've met the Descenders."

"The *who*?" Noah said.

"The Descenders," Mr. Darby repeated. "Tameron, Hannah—"

Tameron interrupted, saying, "We didn't mention that."

"Hmmm." Mr. Darby touched a finger to his lips, and his forehead wrinkled. "I suppose there will be plenty of time for words. During the training, I mean."

With no hint of enthusiasm, Sam nodded in agreement.

"Training?" said Ella. Concern furrowed her brow, and she glanced at her friends. "Am I missing something here? Did I, like, fall asleep and miss five minutes of the conversation?"

Mr. Darby smiled. Then he stepped in front of the animals that the scouts were sitting on. He reached out and stroked the heads of Blizzard and Little Bighorn.

The two animals nudged against his palms lovingly.

"I apologize, scouts. I'm jumping ahead. I haven't mentioned my proposition—the very reason I asked you here today."

"Proposition?" said Megan.

"I'll put it very simply." Mr. Darby clasped his hands behind his back and spent a moment rocking on his feet. Finally, he touched the snouts of Blizzard and Little Bighorn, leaned forward, and whispered, "How would the four of you like to join us"—he frowned—"in preventing the end of the world?"

CHAPTER 8

A PROPOSITION AT THE FOUNTAIN FORUM

The scouts were silent. They sat perfectly still atop Blizzard and Little Bighorn. In the group around Mr. Darby, only the prairie dogs moved, continuously stirring up leaves as they dashed around the ankles of the polar bear and the rhino.

For Noah, Mr. Darby's words jarred a memory of the scouts' first meeting with Tank, outside of Creepy Critters. At that time, Tank alluded to someone being in danger, and when Richie asked who, Tank simply replied, "Everyone—the whole world." Now, two weeks later, Mr. Darby had insinuated the same thing.

Hannah finally ended the silence by popping a bubble and letting the gum smack her mouth. She licked the thin, sticky paste from her lips.

"Ooo-kay," said Richie, his voice quivering. "All this talk from you guys about the world ending and stuff—it's really starting to freak me out."

"I'm with Richie," said Noah.

"Understandably," answered Mr. Darby. "It comes with the territory of our plight."

Ella said, "Let's hear this proposition—the one where we help save the world."

The old man whisked his book off his chair and plopped back into the cushions. He swept one side of his trench coat over his legs and flattened the wrinkles with his palm. Noah found it a bit odd that he would cover himself. Could he possibly be cold?

"Over the past two weeks, I've spoken at great length with the Secret Council, and we have unanimously decided to offer you the opportunity to become Crossers."

"Crossers . . ." said Noah. "You mentioned this the last time we were here. What exactly is a Crosser?"

Mr. Darby gathered his bushy beard in his hand and stroked it to a point. "A Crosser, in its simplest terms, is someone who passes between our zoos—the Clarksville Zoo and the Secret Zoo. A Crosser can *cross* from one zoo to the other, *cross* an entire sector, or *cross* from a sector into the City of Species."

"Like we just did," said Ella. "Through Metr-APE-olis."

"Exactly so." Mr. Darby continued to stroke his beard. "As you know, the Clarksville Zoo exhibits have hidden entrances to different sectors of the Secret Zoo—sectors that connect to the City of Species, the core of our kingdom. Though these entrances were made for animals, our human Crossers use them, too. A Crosser's biggest responsibility is to guard these entrances, which we call sector gateways, or simply gateways. To do this successfully, Crossers are trained to effectively cross any sector."

"Are they all human?" Richie asked. "The Crossers, I mean."

"Not at all." Mr. Darby turned to Megan. "Remember the monkeys you spotted on the rooftops of your neighborhood when this all began?"

Megan nodded. "They weren't supposed to be there, right? They snuck out of the zoo?"

Mr. Darby couldn't restrain a smile. "Oh, they snuck out of the zoo, but they most certainly were supposed to be there. They were Crossers—Crossers that patrol the border of the Clarksville Zoo. Some animals post in the trees of your neighborhood at night. We—"

"Whoa!" Ella said. "Did you just say *they post in our trees?*"

Mr. Darby nodded. "Indeed."

"Since when?" Ella asked.

"Since long before you were born."

"What?"

Mr. Darby laughed, then said, "We post tarsiers, mostly. But others as well. Our world invades yours once yours falls to darkness."

"Way, way, *way* cool!" said Richie.

Noah steered the topic back. "How many Crossers are people?"

"Not many. Most people are dedicated to the Inside or the Outside. Most don't have the courage to cross."

Richie said, "And what makes you think we do?"

"Seeing is believing."

"Huh?"

"You crossed through Little Dogs of the Prairie, Penguin Palace, and the Chamber of Lights—without even knowing how to! Don't think this happened without the notice of the Secret Council."

"Yeah, but we were—"

"On top of that, we just put you through a test—a test you passed very smoothly, I should add."

"What?" said Noah. "A test?"

"The Secret Metr-APE-olis," said Mr. Darby. "That test

was proposed by the Secret Council. I apologize for not announcing it beforehand, but Council insisted that the four of you not know." Mr. Darby glanced at Tank. "How many prospective Crossers would you say fail to cross the Secret Metr-APE-olis?"

Tank smiled, and his perfect teeth gleamed like pearls against his dark skin. "Don't know. But most of them, that's for sure."

Mr. Darby turned back to the scouts. "Not many people have the emotional strength to swing across a forest from the arms of apes, I assure you. Yet, the four of you crossed with ease. Most didn't think you would." Mr. Darby gestured toward Sam and his companions. "Even our young Descenders doubted your ability."

Noah wondered if this was partly why the Descenders didn't like them—because the scouts had proven them wrong.

"Hold on," Ella chimed in. "Your Crossers don't seem to be doing such a great job of things. Nobody stopped *us* from sneaking into the Secret Zoo a few weeks ago."

Mr. Darby laughed and said, "That's because the animals protecting the sector gateways wanted you in—to find Megan and solve the mystery of her disappearance. Think about it. The prairie dogs, Podgy, Blizzard, Little Bighorn—they're all Crossers, and they all wanted you inside."

"That makes sense," said Megan. "But what about me? I was able to sneak in."

"Which made only the second time our borders were breached," said Mr. Darby. "Not so bad, given our history."

"Who breached your borders the first time?" Richie asked.

Mr. Darby frowned at the thought. "We're about to get to that."

Megan shifted the conversation back, saying, "How come I wasn't noticed when I came through the Chamber of Lights? Who was guarding that exhibit?"

"Charlie Red. And I assure you, his work is normally exceptional. But that day, Charlie had stepped away from his post to investigate a noise outside the exhibit. By the time he returned, it was too late. You were in."

"So that's why he can't stand us," Ella said. "We made him look like a dork."

"Perhaps there's some truth in that," said Mr. Darby. "No one likes to look incapable of doing his job."

A moment passed without question or comment. Then Mr. Darby continued. "Regarding our Crossers, we need more humans. We especially need people to concentrate on the Outside—people who can walk our borders in the Clarksville Zoo without raising eyebrows. People who know the surrounding neighborhood, its residents and properties. People who can cross quickly into the Secret Zoo during an emergency."

Megan chuckled nervously. "Mr. Darby . . . we're kids! We have families. And school."

"Yeah," said Ella. "I have to think that life gets pretty tough for someone who quits the books in fifth grade."

Mr. Darby leaned over his knees. "We aren't suggesting that you give up your lives. Only that you help us in your free time—that you train with us and be alert for unusual activity on the Outside, especially in your neighborhood. Our ability to watch activities on your streets is limited, especially during the day."

"Train with you?" said Ella. "Do you have any idea how hard it was for Megan just to get permission to come to the zoo this morning?"

"Training wouldn't take the time you might imagine. Maybe two hours, twice a week. Much of the training would take place in the Clarksville Zoo, making it that much easier for you."

The scouts glanced at one another and silently considered the proposition. Noah thought about how the Clarksville Zoo was in their neighborhood, right between their houses and their school. After a bit, Noah asked, "How would it work?"

"The Secret Council has proposed that Tank lead

your training. He'll be assisted by the Descenders. Sam, Tameron, Hannah, and Solana are four of the strongest, most capable Crossers we have. You would train slowly, on weekends, evenings, or any days that you have available."

"But what would we tell our parents?" Ella asked. "How would we get out of the house?"

Mr. Darby looked at Tank, whose smile was broader than ever. The big man reached into a duffel bag beside his chair and pulled out a wad of shirts in the clutch of his massive hand. One by one, he tossed a shirt to each of the scouts. "You'd say this."

Noah opened his shirt and laid it on the back of Blizzard's head. A button-up with vertical stripes, it had an enormous collar that reached across the shoulders. The left side had two patches; one had the words CLARKSVILLE ZOO in loopy cursive writing, and the other read NOAH. The right side had a breast pocket large enough to fit a *Harry Potter* paperback. It was the ugliest shirt Noah had ever seen.

"Coooool!" Richie gushed as he buried his entire hand in the pocket. "It has a ton of space for my pens and stuff!"

Ella rolled her eyes. "A nerd and his nerd gear."

"What would we do with these?" Noah asked.

"You'd work for us," said Mr. Darby. "Only a few hours a week, of course."

Richie raised one eyebrow. "You wouldn't . . . like . . . expect us to clean the cages or something, would you? I mean, the elephants! Have you seen the size of their . . . you know . . . poop?"

"You don't get it, Richie," Noah said. "Mr. Darby doesn't want us to work for the zoo. He wants us to make it seem like we're working for the zoo. We'll actually be training."

"Exactly!" Mr. Darby said. "We call it crosstraining. But to your families, we could easily mask it as volunteering. As you probably know, the Clarksville Zoo offers volunteer opportunities to students at the local schools. It's a perfect way to present your training as something acceptable to your parents."

"How long would the training take?" Noah asked.

"Since you'd only be training a few hours a week . . . a number of years."

"Great," said Ella. "There goes my soccer career."

Tameron suddenly stepped forward. "I can't take this anymore!" He faced Mr. Darby and waved an arm toward the scouts. "They're just kids! Kids from the Outside—which is even worse! Yeah, they can cross—I'll give them that—but they don't have what it takes. They haven't seen what we've seen. They're not Insiders, Mr. Darby. They weren't here the day the shadows were taken!"

Tameron fell silent. As he turned away, the sunlight struck his jacket at an unusual angle. Noah noticed that the pleats had thin cuts in the bottom of the folds. He wondered if there was a reason for the cuts, but before he had time to study them, the Descender moved out of the light, and they were concealed once more.

A prickly silence hung in the air. It was the first awkward moment the scouts had shared with Mr. Darby.

Finally, Noah voiced what all the scouts were thinking. "What was 'the day the shadows were taken'?"

Tank shifted in his chair. Hannah stopped blowing air into her bubble, and the pink globe seemed to float in front of her face. The prairie dogs stopped racing and stood on their haunches, their attention switching from Noah to Mr. Darby and back again.

Sam took a step toward Mr. Darby. "You don't have to answer that. Remember, we're talking to Outsiders here."

Mr. Darby locked eyes with Sam. For a moment, all that seemed to exist was the contemplative aura about the old man. The splashing water in the fountain made the only sounds.

Finally, Mr. Darby turned and faced the scouts. "If you wish to know the history of the stolen shadows, it will require your full engagement in our plight. We will need you as Crossers, and we will need you not only to be brave, but to be fearless." Mr. Darby paused, giving the scouts time to digest his words. "I want you to think before answering. Can you accept the challenge to become one of us? To join our society as Crossers who live on the Outside?"

In silence, the scouts traded glances, their eyes communicating more information than words ever could.

At last, Noah said, "If it means helping you—and if it means helping others—then, yes, we accept your invitation to join the Secret Society."

Megan, Ella, and Richie nodded in agreement.

Solana turned to Mr. Darby and said, "You can't be serious! They don't know what they're getting into. They're kids! Think of their parents! What if their parents—"

Mr. Darby raised his palm to silence her. The corners of his mouth curled in a smile, and the old man tipped his head at Noah to show his gratitude. Sitting atop a dreadfully powerful polar bear, Noah nodded back.

"Then, welcome." The usual emotion had drained from Mr. Darby's voice. "Welcome to our Secret Society."

Blizzard rolled back his head and roared so thunderously that the earth shook, the bookcases rumbled, and every creature in the library held on to branches or furniture to keep from falling. Leaves rained down, flashing color across the magical landscape.

The old man smiled—a smile that was both warm and wicked. He wrestled his aged body into a comfortable position in the chair. Then he set his eyes on the scouts and began to tell a tale.

CHAPTER 9

KAVITA AND KHUFU

"Before I tell you about the Taking of the Shadows, you need to understand a piece of history not taught in the books of your schools. Magic is real, and it comes from the only true magician who has ever existed. She lived around 2500 B.C."

"She was a girl?" Ella asked, surprised. "That totally rocks!"

"She was indeed a girl—a woman, more accurately. She was born in India, and her name was Kavita."

Noah's brow furrowed. The name sounded familiar. He searched his memory but couldn't place it; as Mr. Darby continued his story, he pushed the thought aside.

"At an early age, Kavita recognized her talent, but she kept it a secret. She could move things with her mind. Magic! Her magic had but one requirement—starlight. It would work only when the light of the moon or stars shone on her body. In daylight, she was powerless."

Richie raised his hand and wiggled his fingers.

"Yes, Richie?"

"How do you know this stuff? I mean, ancient history doesn't have a lot of details."

"Yeah," said Ella. "It's not like Kavita kept a blog."

Mr. Darby couldn't suppress his smile. "For now, just know that we know. In the end, you'll know everything, too."

This was enough to satisfy Richie. He nodded.

Mr. Darby continued. "When Kavita was a young woman, she traveled across India and Arabia and down into Egypt. Her travels ended near the village of Giza, on the western bank of the Nile River. There she came upon the construction of the Great Pyramid of Giza."

"Too cool!" said Richie. "Imagine stumbling across something like that!"

"Certainly it wasn't an everyday sight—especially some 4,500 years ago. Kavita headed toward the pyramid— this mysterious and magnificent structure that rose from the earth—and made her way into a quarry."

"A what?" said Ella.

Richie explained before Mr. Darby could reply. "It's a place where stone is taken from the earth. It usually looks like a huge pit with stone walls. I'm guessing the quarry that Kavita found was supplying stone for the Great Pyramid."

"Exactly," said Mr. Darby. "And it was quite a sight. Hundreds of men standing along the ledges of the walls, pounding chisels into the stone. Huge blocks falling to the ground. Men rolling slabs of stone onto wooden sledges and pulling them across the sandy floor.

"As Kavita moved across the quarry, the workers stopped their efforts to stare. One worker ran up, seized her wrist, and dragged her away to the north side of the pyramid, where a regal man stood dressed in long white robes and attended by servants. Seeing Kavita, the man paled with disbelief, then took her away."

Mr. Darby paused and shifted in his seat. Behind him the fountain sprayed, sending thin clouds of mist into the air. "Kavita was taken to a hut in a nearby village. There, she waited. Once the sun had made way for the stars to shine, a man entered. Kavita could tell by his flashy garb and stiff posture that he was an important person—a king to the others. History tells us now that King Khufu was his name. Khufu pointed to the sky, to himself, to Kavita, and then in the direction of the pyramid. Then, still explaining, he dropped his forehead to the sand before raising his face to the stars in a gesture of prayer. And Kavita understood."

"Understood what?" Ella said. "You're losing me."

"Khufu had prayed to the heavens for help with his pyramid, and he believed the heavens had delivered her to him."

"Wow!" said Richie. "Imagine someone thinking you're a gift from the gods to a king!"

Noah still wondered about the name *Kavita*. He knew he had heard it before. He was about to ask Mr. Darby about it when the old man continued his story.

"Khufu engaged Kavita with his crew. She took over the job of moving and setting the stones in the pyramid—something she did at night by using her magic. Every evening the workmen left hundreds of giant blocks strewn across the quarry. And every morning they woke to find the quarry empty and hundreds of new stones set in place. Over time, this created a problem for the workmen."

"A problem?" said Megan. "Why?"

"The workers believed that in creating the pyramid, they were preparing themselves for acceptance into the afterlife. While Khufu was certain that Kavita had come from the heavens, many workers were not. Some feared her. And they feared that Kavita's work, when viewed by the gods, would minimize their own efforts. Would this prevent their welcome into the heavens?

"One night, many months after Kavita's arrival, a group of workers slipped from their huts and escaped to the pyramid under the cover of darkness. They were armed with the hammers and copper rods that they used in the quarry. They climbed the ramp to the top of the pyramid, several hundred feet above ground, found Kavita, and stopped in their tracks. With her arms raised, Kavita was using magic to slide the blocks into place. All around her, the massive stones shifted and turned, as if jostling for position in the rows of the pyramid.

"The workers inched toward Kavita. They felt they had to stop her. As they closed in, Kavita noticed them. She ran to an open spot and fought them off by hurling the great stones at them. Some workmen were crushed, and others were thrown to the distant desert floor. When only five were left standing, something terrible happened. Kavita stepped into a hole and dropped thirty feet into the pyramid."

Ella interrupted the story. "A hole? What are you talking about? Why would—"

"She landed in the tunnel leading to the king's chamber. The tunnel, called the Grand Gallery, is the biggest, most elaborate part of the pyramid's tunnel system.

Kavita was constructing it by leaving an open space for it—an open space into which she fell."

"What happened?" Megan asked. "The men—did they—"

"Come after her? Yes, I'm afraid they did. In the darkness, Kavita heard their bare feet thumping the stone floor. And in the long, confined space of the Grand Gallery, she had no way to escape. She was trapped in the pyramid."

"But her magic!" Ella shouted. "Why didn't she—?"

"The starlight couldn't find the deep, dark trench of the Gallery. With no celestial light, she couldn't work her magic. She became as powerless as you or I. Kavita ran until she finally reached the bottom chamber, where the tunnel came to an end. There, in the underground chamber of the Great Pyramid, the crazed men claimed the life of the world's only magician."

The scouts cringed on the backs of their animal friends. Noah felt sick—and for Kavita's sake, he felt betrayed.

"How could they do it?" Ella asked. "The men—how could they be so cruel?"

Mr. Darby shook his head. "Fear. The emotion that controls us best."

"Did they get caught—the men?" Megan asked.

"I don't know. But one thing is certain. Khufu learned of Kavita's murder, and fearing retaliation from the gods, he had his crew add two open shafts connecting the top chamber of the pyramid to the open air outside. The purpose of the shafts was to release Kavita's magic back to the heavens, the place he believed it belonged."

"Did . . . did it work?" Ella asked.

"Yes and no," said Mr. Darby. "They released Kavita's magic, but not to the heavens. For the last 4,500 years, this magic—an energy that eludes the science of your world—has continued to rise out of the darkness from the deep bottom chamber of the Great Pyramid, filling the world's shadows with unimaginable power untouched by all of civilization."

Like everything else about the Secret Zoo, Kavita's story was almost too extraordinary to believe. No one made a sound—not the scouts, not the Descenders, not Tank, and none of the animals. Then Noah saw his opportunity to ask the question that had been bothering him.

"Kavita," Noah said. "That name—I've heard it before. Where?"

"You have indeed heard it before," Mr. Darby said. "Kavita was the name of a remarkable mother whom I've told you about."

Noah searched his memory. "I don't know . . . I can't place it."

"Two weeks ago I shared with you the story of how the Secret Zoo was created. It required the magic of identical triplets from India—three brothers. Their names were Bhanu, Kavi, and Vishal. You will remember that these brothers were born of different mothers, in different cities, at exactly the same time. The mothers all shared the same name."

Noah gasped. For several moments, he couldn't catch his breath. When he finally did, he could only manage a single word—the only word that mattered: "Kavita."

Mr. Darby nodded. Then, gravely, he said, "It's a complicated part of the story, and none of us understands it completely. All we know is that the brothers, when joined together, could reach into the shadows of the world, take Kavita's magic, and use it."

Noah had just enough breath to whisper, "And they used it to create the Secret Zoo."

ᴄᴋ CHAPTER 10 ᏥᏋ

The Taking of the Shadows

No one spoke. Noah forced himself to breathe.

After a long silence, Mr. Darby said, "I know it's complicated and strange, but let me continue. Soon it will make more sense. For now, let me tell you about the day the shadows were taken." The old man sat straight in his chair. "I was in the City of Species on the day it happened: April fifteenth in the year 1927. At some point in the evening, a commotion broke in the street. The source? A man. A man in a dark, flowing trench coat and a fedora hat with a wide brim. He'd emerged from a velvet curtain of a sector and walked into the city.

"He was so dreadfully strange that our Secret Cityzens saw him at once. The brim of his hat cast a shadow across his eyes, like a mask. Most of his face was hidden behind the upturned collar of his jacket. His skin, pasty white, looked as though it had never been touched by the sun. His lips were so dry and cracked that they gave the appearance of dead, shriveled worms. Of his body, nothing was visible but his hands. Plump blue veins crawled along them, winding around his knotted knuckles. Black, swollen nails curled off his fingertips. He had a dreadful aura, and the Secret Cityzens feared him at once. As he brushed by, they jumped out of his path.

"As he headed across the city, the Secret Cityzens began to realize that parts of their shadows were breaking away into his. He seemed to be sweeping them off the street. As the missing pieces quickly reappeared, the darkness in the man's shadow grew more and more absolute. It was as if their shadows were pooling into his, thickening it.

"After some time, a bloodcurdling scream split the air. All heads turned to the sound. Near a sector, a man had dropped to his knees, clutching his head. It was Bhanu, one of the magical brothers. People ran to his aid and draped their arms around his shoulders, trying to comfort him. Confused by his pain, Bhanu pushed them aside and kept screaming.

"While this was happening, the man in the trench coat walked on. He passed new people and new animals, claiming parts of their shadows for his own. His shadow began to thicken like a fog—a thing with weight and density, rather than an area simply vacant of light. And like a fog, this shadow began to move and churn and rise from the street. It seemed to come alive.

"Another scream ripped across the city. A few blocks away, another man had fallen to his knees, like Bhanu, clutching his head in pain. It was Vishal. People were terrified—something was happening to the brothers! The Secret Cityzens became unsure of everything."

The scouts hung on every word, silent and puzzled. At the feet of Blizzard and Little Bighorn, the prairie dogs whimpered softly.

"The man in the trench coat continued forward, drawing more and more shadows into his own. Trails of darkness swirled around his boots and wafted up his legs. They engulfed his black trench coat and curled around his pale neck. As the shadows reached his face, he began to breathe them in. Darkness streamed in and out of his mouth. He seemed to draw energy from their sudden substance—like oxygen, the shadows seemed to offer him life.

"From down the street came another scream. This time it was Kavi, Bhanu's other brother. He collapsed to his side, writhing in pain, his legs kicking out at the nothingness around him.

"The man walked on, the fog around him swirling and rising. His arms and legs stirred the darkness. He continued to draw the shadows into his lungs, like air. And like air, the shadows began to affect his body as they coursed through it. The map of plump veins across his hands turned black. Dark blotches formed on his face. His dry lips darkened and grayed.

"A group of Secret Cityzens were terrified into action. But as they converged on the man, he took off running, surrounded by his foggy shadow. He tore through the crowd, turned down a long alley, and vanished into its half darkness, his body seeming to dissipate. Shortly after he was gone, the brothers stopped screaming and rose to their feet, confused and stunned."

Mr. Darby stopped and looked gravely at each of the scouts. Then the old man rose from his chair and strolled over to Noah, his long coat trailing behind him, a bit like a king's gown. Beneath the weighty velvet, crisp, colorful leaves crumbled to pieces. When he reached Noah, he laid his open palm against Blizzard's head. The mighty bear rolled his face into Mr. Darby's touch and softly sniffed his sleeve.

In a flat, serious voice, Mr. Darby said, "It was him. The one we call the Shadowist."

Richie quivered. "Okay, this Shadowist dude . . . yeah, kind of creepy. So if you could explain—"

Mr. Darby said, "He is the one who lives among the shadows—who draws breath from them."

"But who is he?" Noah asked. "Where did he come from?"

"Outside," said Mr. Darby. "The outside world—your world."

"How did he get in?"

"He crossed. We don't know how or through which sector, but we know that at least once he crossed and discovered our Secret Zoo and the City of Species." Mr. Darby crouched and the prairie dogs scurried up to him, gathering around his ankles. He stroked a few of their heads.

"But how do you know he wasn't a Secret Cityzen from the Inside?" Ella asked.

"It's something we just know—partly from reason, partly from intuition."

For a moment, no one said a word. Mr. Darby fixed his stare on Noah, who saw himself reflected in each dark lens of the old man's sunglasses.

"Months after the shadows were taken, some people spotted a strange man in the Secret Zoo and chased him outside. They described him as wearing a long black coat and a big hat with a wide, circular brim—a fedora hat. Only one person was able to get a good look at this stranger: the guard at the front gates of the Clarksville Zoo. This guard saw the stranger's face—or what should have been his face, anyway. Parts of it were missing."

"Missing?" said Noah.

"His nose, his cheek . . . parts of the stranger were simply . . . gone. His flesh seemed held together by darkness." Mr. Darby stared at the scouts before continuing. "Many are certain that this was the man who had walked down the City of Species, drawing shadows into his own. The stranger did more than take our shadows—he *became* them. He became darkness itself—all that is not."

"This is crazy!" Ella was suddenly exasperated with the whole story. "How can someone become a shadow? A shadow is nothing! A shadow is a . . . a . . ." She turned to Richie. "Help me out, Little Einstein. What the heck is a shadow?"

"It's . . . nothing, just like you said. It's an area that light can't reach."

Mr. Darby pushed his sunglasses up on his nose. "That's exactly why Kavita's magic stays in the shadows. Shadows escape the light of human understanding. In their darkness, Kavita's magic remains hidden."

"This magic," said Richie, "what's it like?"

"It's an energy. It swirls in the shadows. It spills forth from the Great Pyramid. During the day, visitors unknowingly carry it in their shadows as they walk between the pyramids. Then they leave with the magic, taking it elsewhere."

Noah asked, "But how did the magic get all the way here—to America?"

"A common virus can spread across the earth in a matter of days. Think of the time Kavita's magic has had. In over 4,500 years, her magic has spread everywhere, not just to America."

"Everywhere in the whole world?"

Mr. Darby nodded. "But no one other than the Secret Society knows about it. And the only reason we know is because of Bhanu and his brothers."

"But how—how did Bhanu and his brothers use it?"

Mr. Darby gestured to the surrounding bookcases. "Down these aisles are countless books on the history of the Secret Society. In one, Bhanu described reaching into shadows and feeling the magic swirling there. The feeling, he said, was like a soft, burning sensation that started at his fingertips and crept up his arms and across his chest. His head would explode with light, and he'd feel something churning in his mind. At this point he was able to redefine the properties of his surroundings. Shape them."

Noah listened intently. One thing still didn't make sense.

"How did the Shadowist get to the magic? You said

that Bhanu and his brothers were the only ones who knew about it."

Mr. Darby cleared his throat. "You're right. I did say that."

"Okay. Then what about the Shadowist?"

"The Shadowist has a name. Jonathan DeGraff."

"DeGraff . . ." said Richie. "That name . . . where have I heard it before?"

With his attention still fixed on Mr. Darby, Noah was the one who answered. "In the story of Mr. Jackson, the man who created the Clarksville Zoo. DeGraff was the guy who told Mr. Jackson about Bhanu and his brothers so that Mr. Jackson would go to them to create the Secret Zoo."

"Yes," said Mr. Darby. "But I'm afraid there is more to that story. DeGraff is the fourth identical brother."

Noah's heart dropped.

Mr. Darby continued. "Once DeGraff found his way into the Secret Zoo—once he neared his three brothers— he, too, was able to reach into the shadows and use Kavita's magic. And he used it to draw the shadows into his body, to become their very substance—dark, empty, eternal."

Ella said, "But the other brothers are dead now. Why does it matter if the Shadowist gets back inside the Secret Zoo?"

Mr. Darby said, "Though the other brothers are dead, their power is not."

Hearing this, Noah remembered what Mr. Darby had told them during their first adventure in the Secret Zoo. He had said that the brothers' magic was still alive, and the Secret Society still used it.

"But how—"

"The Cemetery Sector," said Mr. Darby.

Noah nodded. "One of the Forbidden Five. The Descenders just told us about it."

"The three brothers are buried there in a single casket. Their bodies still draw the magic from the shadows."

"So if the Shadowist gets near the Cemetery Sector . . ." Noah's voice trailed off.

Mr. Darby finished his thought. "If the Shadowist gets near the Cemetery Sector, he'll draw enough power and magic into himself to destroy the entire Secret Society and then move on to your world."

The idea struck Noah with such force that he shuddered. For the first time, he truly understood what the Secret Society was up against.

"But why?" Megan asked. "Why does DeGraff want to do this? Why is he so wicked?"

"Soon you will know," Mr. Darby said. The old man paused and became more serious than ever. "But in the end, you'll wish to forget."

◆€ CHAPTER 11 €◆

THE PLAN

Mr. Darby sat once again in the pillowed chair beside the fountain and crossed his legs, his long purple coat spilling over the leafy floor. The prairie dogs, more frightened than ever, gathered in its velvet folds, yipping weakly.

Mr. Darby murmured, "There, there." He scooped the prairie dogs up two at a time and set them gently on the wide arms of the chair and his lap. "They frighten easily," he said, the suggestion of a smile on his lips.

Ella jerked her thumb over her shoulder in Richie's direction. "They're not the only ones." After he'd heard the story of the Shadowist, Richie's face was almost as white as Blizzard's fur.

Megan said to Mr. Darby, "Something doesn't make sense. The Shadowist . . . how did he—"

Mr. Darby stopped her with a raised hand. "I will say nothing more about him today. During your crosstraining, you'll learn more about DeGraff—more than you'll care to know. In the end, the story will haunt you as it haunts us all."

"Sounds great," Richie squeaked. "Sounds like something I'll look forward to. You know—like summer vacation."

"For now," said Mr. Darby, "let's return our attention to your crosstraining."

"When do we begin?" Noah asked.

Mr. Darby scratched P-Dog's head. "As soon as possible."

"Okay, but how?" Noah held up the ugly shirt with the big collar, his recent gift from Tank. "I mean, you gave us these, but what—"

"I'll let Tank address that."

Tank leaned forward. "So, you guys are pretty sure your parents will be cool about you volunteering at the zoo?"

The scouts traded stares.

"I think so," Noah said. "It's hard to guess. Our parents know we love the zoo—I mean, we've lived next to it our whole lives. And they encourage after-school stuff, sports and stuff like that. But with Megan's disappearance, everyone's still kind of freaking out." He turned to his sister. "Meg, what do you think?"

"If we can convince them that the four of us will always be volunteering together, I think they'll go for it."

"Okay," said Tank, "then I think this will work." He picked up a stack of pamphlets beside his chair and tossed one at each of the scouts. "Volunteer brochures. For the Clarksville Zoo. Show them to your folks and find something you'd like to pretend to be." As the scouts leafed through the brochures, he continued, "On cross-training days, you guys will get dressed in your . . ." He caught sight of Noah's shirt and searched for the right words. "Man, those things are ugly! Mr. D, who picked those nasty things out?"

Mr. Darby pointed to the Descenders, who were smiling half wickedly.

"Figures," Ella whispered to her friends.

The big man pried his eyes away from Noah's shirt and went on. "Anyway, you guys will get dressed in those ugly shirts and come down to the Clarksville Zoo—any time of day, any day of the week, it doesn't matter—and we'll train you. Some of the training will take place in the Clarksville Zoo, and some will take place in the Secret Zoo, in the sectors and the City of Species." Tank jabbed his thumb at the Descenders. "These bad-looking dudes over here are going to be doing most of the crosstraining. I'll be instructing them. You'll learn how to slip into the Secret Zoo in the middle of the day during the busiest weeks of the year. You'll learn how to use the animals to cross the sectors in record time. At the end of your crosstraining, you'll be able to cross from anywhere in the Clarksville Zoo to the City of Species in less than ten minutes. Always. No exceptions. For a Crosser, speed is critical."

"This is going to be *way* cool," said Megan.

Mr. Darby said, "Blizzard, Little Bighorn, Podgy, and P-Dog will be permanently assigned to you throughout your development as Crossers."

A wave of excitement rippled through the scouts. Noah held out his palm toward Podgy in a high five, but the penguin only stared blankly at his hand.

Mr. Darby continued. "As for Marlo, he'll serve as a messenger between us all. I'll have him check in with you periodically to see if you have messages for me or anyone else in the Secret Society." He paused. "Crosstraining will be difficult, I assure you. You'll need to maintain your lives on the Outside and not raise suspicion. This will be especially difficult with your parents. You are being tasked with a great responsibility, one that carries a high degree of honor in our Secret Society. Knowing your heart and character, I am certain you will respect this."

The scouts nodded.

"Now, assuming your parents permit you to volunteer at the zoo, when can you begin?"

The scouts huddled together. Whispers flew.

"Tuesday," Noah said as he turned back to Mr. Darby. "I think we can do it then. That will give us a few days to talk to our parents. From there, we can arrange other times, a couple of hours after school, or whatever."

Mr. Darby and Tank smiled and nodded. Excited, Blizzard growled, Little Bighorn grunted, and Podgy waddled in place. Everyone was enthusiastic—everyone but the Descenders, who simply stood there, showing no emotion at all. They were careful not to look at the scouts. Hannah stared at her nails; Solana at the fallen leaves; Tameron at the fountain; Sam at a monkey high atop a bookcase.

"Now then," said Mr. Darby as he rose from the chair, softly sweeping the prairie dogs from his lap. "Let's get you home." The old man extended his arms to Blizzard and Little Bighorn. "Might the two of you assist our newest members of the Secret Society back to the Clarksville City Zoo?"

Blizzard and Little Bighorn turned and lumbered back among the towering bookshelves. The prairie dogs returned to their familiar shenanigans, darting in circles and tunneling through the leaves. The Descenders, Mr. Darby, and Tank followed.

As the motley group crossed the Library of the Secret Society, eyes lifted to watch their steady path toward the exit doors. Monkeys stopped stacking books and stared. It seemed to Noah that everyone in the library knew what had just occurred—that Mr. Darby had invited the scouts to join the Secret Society.

Blizzard and Little Bighorn poked their snouts through the dangling beads at the exit and plodded out onto the landing, high above the streets of the City of Species. There, the magnificence of the scene that greeted the scouts rivaled anything they had encountered so far.

CHAPTER 12

THE CHICKADEE CEREMONY

Around the Library of the Secret Society, an immense gathering of animals erupted in noise. Hooves clattered and paws thudded on the hard streets. Growls and grunts ricocheted off the city walls. Squawks descended from the partial canopy of colorful leaves.

Noah turned to Richie. "Gee," he teased, "think they know what just happened?"

Richie was too stunned for words. His mouth hung open in an oval of surprise, his eyes as large and round as quarters.

Leaves and mist rained down over the scouts as they

sat perched on Blizzard and Little Bighorn at the top of the staircase. The animals covered the streets, sidewalks, rooftops, awnings, trees—everything. Birds packed the sky, and the strokes of thousands of wings stirred the air. Monkeys dangled from branches, ledges, and lamps, and stood on the backs of bears and hippos. Snakes coiled around posts and railings, flicking out their forked tongues. The building walls seemed to move as geckos and lizards scuttled across them.

Mr. Darby rattled the dangling beads as he stepped out onto the landing. He bellowed with laughter at the spectacle before him.

"They're welcoming you as new members to the Secret Society—and as Crossers!"

"Word spreads pretty quick around here," said Ella.

"Indeed!" said the old man. "Here the gossip truly flies on wings."

Blizzard and Little Bighorn began to lumber down the steep staircase, the scouts lurching on their backs. The animals in their way melted aside to open a path. Blizzard's massive paws threatened to make pancakes out of the smaller animals—chipmunks, turtles, meerkats. To avoid the crowded steps, Podgy took to the air, soaring down the staircase just above the heads of the taller animals. When he reached the street, he veered toward the roof of a tall mailbox and attempted to touch down, but lost his footing on the slippery surface and tumbled over, his flippers flailing.

Noah grinned at the sight. Then he leaned toward Mr. Darby and said, "I don't understand why the animals like us so much."

Walking between Blizzard and Little Bighorn, Mr. Darby replied, "They see something special in you."

"But what?"

"A reflection of the better parts of themselves."

Noah's brow wrinkled. "What's *that* supposed to mean?"

Mr. Darby smiled and said, "You'll let me know when it becomes obvious, yes?"

Sometimes, thought Noah, Mr. Darby didn't make a bit of sense. The old man liked to talk in riddles.

As the group proceeded down the street, a little bird landed on Noah's shoulder right beside Marlo. It was black and white and as round as a ball—a chickadee. Marlo, startled and possessive of his space, pecked at the newcomer, who jumped back. Another chickadee landed on Noah's other shoulder. Noah shared a glance with the chubby bird.

"Hello?" said Noah.

The bird's round head tipped to one side.

A third chickadee landed. Then a fourth. A fifth. They began to touch down everywhere on Noah's body—on his arms, his shoulders, his back, his legs, even on the brim of his cap. In a matter of seconds, Noah was covered. Tiny talons pricked his clothes.

He glanced back at Megan, who looked dressed in chickadees. On Little Bighorn, Ella and Richie were covered, too. The birds perched on their arms and legs, on their backs, on the fluffy pink globes of Ella's earmuffs and the fabric of Richie's red cap. A pair even clung to Richie's glasses.

Still walking between Little Bighorn and Blizzard, Mr. Darby called out to Tank, "The Chickadee Ceremony? So soon?"

Smiling, Tank shrugged his shoulders. "Looks like everybody loves the scouts, Mr. D."

Richie said, "Can someone please tell me what the heck the Chickadee Ceremony is?"

Mr. Darby and Tank erupted with laughter. Finally, Mr. Darby said, "It's the only way for you to meet the animals—all of them!"

"What are you talking about?" asked Richie.

Before Mr. Darby could say any more, the chickadees fluttered their wings and rose into the air, lifting the scouts. Suspended by tiny claws, Noah flew forward, his toes skipping over Blizzard's head. A spasm of excitement rippled through the crowded streets. A hundred animal voices—grunts and growls, hisses and howls—rose as a singular sound. The four groups of chickadees merged together above the heads of the animals, carrying the scouts through the air, side by side. Giraffes ducked their long necks to avoid being hit.

Noah glanced over at his friends. They were flying parallel to the street with their legs straight out behind them and their torsoes dropped, as if floating on invisible beds. Half crazed, Richie was screaming something, but his words were lost in the surrounding noise.

Like so many moments in the Secret Zoo, this one had a dreamlike quality. Buildings of all designs and materials rose around the scouts, their tops too high to see. Trees filled the landscape and animals crowded their branches—possums, snakes, monkeys, lizards, squirrels, owls, and hundreds of other creatures, furry and scaly, that Noah couldn't name. Bright autumn leaves fell like strokes of momentary color across an imaginary canvas. Animals jumped and reached out to the scouts with paws, claws, and wings. At one point, an elephant's flexuous trunk jabbed Noah in the stomach.

Noah realized what the Chickadee Ceremony was. A parade. A spontaneous parade, welcoming the scouts into the Secret Society and its circle of friendship.

Still flying forward, the chickadees started to swerve back and forth across the street. They swung around columns, dipped below vaulted ceilings, and wove through tree limbs. An ostrich's head bumped Noah, and swept off ten of the chickadees. The little birds darted around nervously before finding their perches again.

For the next five minutes, the scouts soared over the streets of the City of Species as the animals kept up their celebration. Podgy joined them, finding a spot between Megan and Noah. Noah noticed the graceful stroke of his flippers and could hardly believe how well his friend was flying. The big, clumsy penguin had learned so much since his first flight with Noah, when the two of them had narrowly escaped the clutches of the sasquatches. Now he soared like a natural, his flippers effortlessly fanning the air. Noah reached out to give Podgy a thumbs-up, and a chickadee jumped to the tip of his thumb, thinking that Noah was providing yet another perch.

The chickadees slowed their flight as they approached the curtain of a sector gateway. Animals opened a spot on the sidewalk—crawling, hopping, and slinking aside. The chickadees landed the scouts in the clearing and then exploded into the air in all directions, leaving the four friends behind.

The scouts stretched the tension out of their arms and legs. They tugged at their pants, adjusted their hats, and dusted tiny black feathers off their jackets. Poor Richie's face was as white as the chickadees' plump underbellies. His big eyeglasses sat crookedly on his nose, and his hat was an inch away from springing off the crown of his head.

Richie muttered, "And so concludes another nightmarish adventure in the story of *Richie and the Secret Zoo.*" He pulled a glob of wet chickadee feathers out of his mouth.

"C'mon, Richie!" said Megan. "That was absolutely the coolest thing ever!"

"Sometimes . . ." said Richie, wriggling to straighten his pants, "sometimes I swear I have no clue what's wrong with you people."

Just then Mr. Darby, Tank, and their animal friends stepped through the crowd into the clearing. Seeing Richie's pale face and obvious discomfort, Tank buckled over with laughter, his massive shoulders rocking.

"C'mon, man!" he said. "They're chickadees!"

At this, everyone laughed—everyone but Richie. When they quieted down, Noah spied a wide banner hanging between two columns at the front of a tall marble building shaped like a massive cathedral. Stitched to it were flowing gold letters that read "*Sector 109.*"

"Sector One-oh-nine, huh? This must be our way home. What's beyond the curtain?"

Mr. Darby patted Blizzard and Little Bighorn and said, "Why don't you answer that for our new Crossers?"

The two animals lowered their hefty bodies to the leaf-littered sidewalk so the scouts could climb on. Once the kids were aboard, they hoisted themselves up and lumbered toward the sector that would take the scouts home.

Mr. Darby said, "I'll have Marlo check on you guys over the next few days. Unless something changes, plan to meet one of us Tuesday afternoon in Butterfly Nets."

Noah nodded.

As Blizzard prepared to push through the curtain, Mr. Darby added, "Oh, and scouts—"

"Yes?" Noah answered.

"Please do what any good scout would do."

"What's that?"

"Come prepared."

"For what?" Noah asked.

Mr. Darby said, "For anything, my dear scouts. For absolutely anything!"

CHAPTER 13

BUTTERFLY NETS

"Are we ready?" asked Megan.

It was Tuesday afternoon. School had just let out, and the scouts were now standing in front of Butterfly Nets, the Clarksville Zoo's butterfly house. Shaped like two intersecting rectangles, the building had gabled glass rooftops. Leafless stems of ivy spread like a web of cracks across the brick walls.

Three days ago, when the scouts had first mentioned volunteering at the zoo, their parents had the usual concerns: What would the children be doing? What kind of hours would they be working? Who would they be with?

The scouts said they'd be volunteering about three or four hours a week and would never be apart from one another. When their parents worried about how they'd get to and from the zoo, the scouts told them they planned to walk together. The scouts had an answer for everything.

Given Megan's recent disappearance, Noah's mom was the most worried of the parents, and the most reluctant to let her children participate.

Less than a month ago, Megan's amazing homecoming had been national news. Everyone had bought the cover story invented by the Secret Society to explain her three-week disappearance. The idea centered on the house-turned-museum where Mr. Jackson—the wealthy businessman who'd built the Clarksville Zoo and was largely responsible for creating the Secret Zoo—had once lived. The basement of the house was connected to a hidden cellar, which had been used in the first years of the Secret Zoo to temporarily shelter animals waiting to enter the hidden part of the zoo. Megan claimed to have accidentally trapped herself there while exploring the museum. The Secret Society had done the rest—creating the impression that a girl had lived in the basement, luckily stockpiled with food and water, for three weeks. Only the Secret Society and the Action Scouts knew the truth—that Megan had spent those harrowing days held hostage by sasquatches in the Dark Lands.

Despite their many concerns and fears, Megan's parents finally decided to support her desire to learn and grow. They permitted her to volunteer at the zoo as long as she promised to never be alone, and to never go anywhere near "that dreadful museum."

Now the scouts stood on the wide stoop of Butterfly Nets. The entrance to the exhibit was blocked by a sign that said, CLOSED FOR CONSTRUCTION! From behind the doors came the faint sound of spinning saws and pounding hammers.

"Shucks!" said Richie, trying to sound disappointed. He spun away from the entrance. "I guess we'll come back another time."

Ella reached out and seized a handful of Richie's jacket. "Hold up!"

"Hold up for what? There's clearly been some kind of miscommunication. After all, it's been a few days since Mr. Darby told us to—"

"Noah," Ella broke in, "you have the key, right? The one Tank gave you?"

"Of course," Noah answered. Under the dark cover of night, Tank had had a cheetah deliver a key to Noah—a key with magical properties that allowed it to melt and fit any lock at the zoo.

Noah glanced over his shoulders: no one was around. He plucked the key from his pocket and eased it into the lock, its jagged edges softening like butter held to a flame. Once inside, it solidified again. Noah turned his wrist and—*pop!*—the door opened.

Everyone but Richie stepped around the sign and slipped through the doorway.

"Nice!" Richie's muffled voice called out from the other side of the door. "I wonder who'll be the first to play catch with a falling rafter!" But within seconds, Richie pulled the heavy door open and wormed his way through, calling, "Guys! Wait up!"

The construction noises they'd heard outside—hammers whacking, saws cutting, compressors pumping—were louder now, yet there was no sign of any work being done. Megan pointed to one of the many trees that grew inside the building. A speaker was mounted in its branches. Usually, it played soft music.

"Look," she said. "The noises—they're a recording."

As the scouts stared at the speaker, a quiet voice spoke behind them. "Boo."

The scouts jumped and spun around. Tameron stood there, his arms crossed, his cap pulled over his eyes.

Tameron shook his head. "Man, if you guys want to make it as Crossers, you got to stop being so jumpy."

"Real funny," said Richie. "I hope you brought four pairs of clean underwear along with that little joke of yours."

Smirking, Tameron turned and walked off, saying, "C'mon—follow me."

As they trailed Tameron, the scouts glanced around. The open space of the building was full of trees, plants, streams, and fountains. The unique characteristic of the exhibit was its enormous nets—they were everywhere, covering everything. They lay across treetops and rocks and misty waterfalls. They dangled like curtains from the glass ceiling to the grassy floor. Because the holes in the nets were big enough to pitch baseballs through, the butterflies didn't risk getting caught. The nets weren't functional; they were decorative, creating a feeling that everything in the exhibit had been captured in huge nets.

Hundreds of butterflies flitted about, their wings blinking open and closed. They darted in erratic paths, perched on flowering shrubs, and rested on leaves. Their vibrant color spotted everything, as if a storm of paint-filled raindrops had just blown through the building.

Walking behind Tameron, Noah had a good look at the military-style backpack slung over his shoulders. The bottom of the long green canvas pack hung below Tameron's waist. Zippers ran across it in all directions, and it was so full that it seemed ready to burst. Bulging pockets covered the entire bag.

Noah nudged Richie and pointed to the pack, whispering, "What do you make of that?"

Richie shrugged and held out his arms. "Nothing."

"Don't you find it a bit weird that he carries that thing around? What the heck could he have in it? It's big enough to fit you!"

Richie considered this, then shrugged a second time.

Tameron led them across a narrow wooden bridge to a clearing where a large whiteboard sat on an easel. Four folding chairs faced the easel, arranged in a semicircle. Slipping his backpack off his shoulders, Tameron stepped up to the whiteboard, grabbed a marker in one hand, and shot off its cap with a flick of his thumb.

"Class in session," he announced. "Find a chair."

The scouts dropped into the seats.

"I want you guys to listen up, because I hate repeating myself. When I have to repeat myself, it means I'm wasting time. And I don't have time to waste."

Richie raised a stiff arm.

Tameron peered at Richie from the shadow of his hat brim. Frowning, he mumbled, "How in the . . ." He stopped himself, forfeiting one remark in favor of a new one. "How could you possibly have a question already?"

Richie wiggled his fingers. "Mr. Tameron—"

Tameron sighed. "Kid, Tameron's my name."

Confused, Richie asked, "You want me to call you Kid Tameron?"

Tameron planted his hands on his hips. "Kid, what's my name?"

"Tameron."

"Then why would I want you to call me Kid Tameron? Do I call you Kid Richie?"

"No." Somewhere above his head, Richie opened a space for his thoughts and stared into it. "But that would be kind of cool, I think."

Tameron took a step toward Richie and said flatly, "Call me Tameron. Not Mr. Tameron. Not Kid Tameron. Nothing but Tameron, okay? You think you got that?"

Richie nodded.

In silence, the two stared at each other, each waiting for something.

"Kid," said Tameron.

"Yeah?"

"What's your question?"

"Uhhh . . ." Richie thought for a minute. He steered his gaze toward the tall glass roof. Finally, he said, "Ummm . . . I . . . I guess I forgot. Sorry."

Tameron shook his head and turned to the other scouts. "Darby's always bragging about how this kid's so smart!"

"He has his moments," said Ella. "The rest . . . well, we kind of think his brain needs to nap between his big Einstein-like thoughts."

"Whatever, man." Tameron paced in front of the

whiteboard. "Listen, let's get back to this. We got a lot to cover. Today we're going to start out with the real basic stuff. We're going to talk about what you need to do to cross quickly, effectively, and"—he dragged out the last word for emphasis—"*quiietlyy.*

"Rule One for a Crosser: Never get spotted. Never. You get caught crossing, and you just might take the 'secret' out of the Secret Zoo, and that can't happen. Am I clear on this?"

The scouts nodded.

"Good. Richie, what's our first rule?"

Richie smiled. "Not to call you Kid Tameron."

When Tameron didn't return the smile, Richie added, "It's a joke."

Tameron still refused to smile.

Richie coughed nervously into his fist. "How come no one ever gets my jokes?"

"Richie?" Tameron repeated.

"Yeah?"

"What's the first rule?"

Very softly, Richie answered, "Don't get spotted crossing."

Tameron nodded once and turned back to the board. With his marker, he scribbled THE GROTTOES.

"Grottoes," he said. "Who knows what this word means?"

Noah, Megan, and Ella turned to Richie, who already had his hand in the air. His fingers wagged as if they were typing on a floating keyboard.

"Go ahead, kid."

"Grottoes are caves or caverns."

"That's right," said Tameron. "Beneath the Clarksville Zoo is an area we call the Grottoes. They're special cave-like tunnels. I don't want you guys anywhere near them."

"Why?" Noah asked.

"Too dangerous. You could get hurt, lost, or worse. The Grottoes are complicated. Only our best Crossers are able to navigate them."

"Will we ever get to see them?" Megan asked.

"Depends. Become some of our best Crossers, then, yeah."

"Where do they go?" Noah asked.

"We're not even going to talk about them."

"Why not!" Noah said. His own irritation surprised him. "How are we supposed to learn—"

Tameron shook his head. "Nuh-uh, kid. The Grottoes are off-limits. When you think of the Grottoes, just think of some place your butt shouldn't be."

"Like a public toilet seat?" Richie said. He scanned the crowd for a response to his joke, found none, and slumped his shoulders.

Tameron continued, "For now, we're going to concentrate on exhibits that have direct paths into the Secret

Zoo. Single tunnels. Crossers call them 'straight drops.' Like the ones Daisy led you to in Metr-APE-olis."

A butterfly touched down on Noah's shoulder. It was covered in bright blue swirly patterns. It softly stroked its wings, fanning Noah's cheeks. A second butterfly settled on the same shoulder, then a third and a fourth. Glancing at the other scouts, Noah realized that butterflies were landing on them as well. One had perched on Ella's fingertip. She lifted it slowly until it was right in front of her eyes.

"Too cool!" she said. Another butterfly touched down on her lap. "Butterflies rock!"

"Uhhh . . . do these things carry disease?" Richie asked nervously. "Like bird flu or anything?" He leaned over the side of his chair, avoiding an enormous butterfly that wanted to land on his chest.

"Tameron?" Ella asked as she studied the butterfly perched on her fingertip. "Why do the animals do this? Land on people and stuff."

"No one knows for sure. A lot of people think maybe it's their way of saying hello. Or maybe it's the same reason a dog lies across your feet—who knows."

"The animals all love Mr. Darby," Ella added.

"That's no lie. Darby's their fav. It's always been that way, and I don't see any reason it'll change."

Tameron allowed the scouts a few seconds to appreciate

the butterflies. Then he steered the conversation back.

"Anyway, let me say it again. No Grottoes. Stay to the straight drops to the sectors."

"How many sectors are there?" Megan asked.

"Hundreds."

"And they all connect to the Clarksville Zoo?"

"Yep. They're sectioned off by velvet curtains."

Ella asked, "Why do they look so much like the exhibits they connect to, only really super big?"

"When Bhanu and his brothers first created the sectors, the sectors took on the characteristics of the exhibits they connected to. It was just the way the magic worked."

"Like the Secret Forest of Flight," said Ella, "or the Secret Metr-APE-olis. They look a lot like the normal exhibits—only they're massive!"

"Exactly," said Tameron. "Think of each exhibit as having a giant twin. The twins are the sectors. Make sense?"

The scouts nodded.

"Good Crossers can get across any sector to the City of Species in less than ten minutes."

"That's got to be humanly impossible!" said Richie.

"Maybe," answered Tameron. "But you're forgetting one thing."

"What's that?"

"With the help of the animals, Crossers aren't bound to being human."

For the next two hours, Tameron briefed the scouts on the basics of crossing. He steered all talk away from the Grottoes and focused on the straight drops into the Secret Zoo. Tameron told the four friends that the connecting points to the sectors were called "sector gateways," or just "gateways." He said that the gateways were protected by two lines of defense—one line of humans and one of animals. Each line brought its own advantages, and the lines worked best when they worked together.

Noah's stare occasionally shifted to Tameron's backpack. It lay several feet away from the whiteboard, all bulk and weight and canvas. Noah saw the velvet patches along it and remembered what Solana had told them about the bookcases with the same patches. *They adjust,* she had said. Did that mean the backpack would adjust? If so, how?

Tameron went on to list the exhibits that had direct connections to the Secret Zoo—straight drops. As he spoke, he scribbled notes and pictures on the whiteboard. All throughout the lecture, butterflies drifted down from the trees like bright autumn leaves, landing on the scouts' shoulders, arms, backs, and legs. They'd perch, rest their wings for a bit, and flutter back to their normal butterfly business.

The first day's crosstraining was drawing to a close. At

the end, as Tameron was wiping the whiteboard clean, a sudden noise alarmed them. Footfalls.

Tameron and the scouts jerked their heads up and listened. The sound was coming from somewhere behind the trees.

"What's that?" Richie gasped.

"I don't know," Tameron answered.

Noah's heart lurched. The footfalls grew louder. The unknown something was charging straight toward them.

CHAPTER 14
THE UNKNOWN SOMETHING

ameron surprised Noah by dropping the eraser that he'd been holding and stepping in front of the scouts. He faced the sound and spread his arms out to his sides, shielding Noah and his friends. Despite whatever low regard Tameron might have had for the scouts, he was prepared to defend them.

Over his shoulder, Tameron said, "Don't move!"

The scouts didn't.

Tameron did a strange thing then. He reached down, snatched up his immense backpack, and slung it over his shoulders. He fixed the long pack firmly in place.

The rustle of leaves drew closer and closer. Butterflies were everywhere now, fluttering wildly throughout the glassy heights of the exhibit.

Noah's eyes swelled with disbelief as he realized that Tameron's backpack was moving. Inside it, something shifted and rolled from one side to the other. It was as if something in the backpack had come alive.

Just then, the trees and shrubs in front of them parted, and an enormous man jumped over the rail into the clearing. Struggling for breath, he leaned forward and pressed his hands against his knees. Sunlight beamed off his bald head.

"Tank!" Tameron gasped. "What's happening? What's—"

The big man stopped him with a raised hand. "Trouble . . ." he panted. "We had . . . trouble . . . in one of the sectors. . . ."

Tank's left eye was swollen shut, and blood was coming from a long cut on the side of his head. Noah ducked under Tameron's outstretched arm and stood in front of his friend.

"You're hurt!" Noah exclaimed.

Tank raised his hand as he had done with Tameron a moment before, stopping Noah.

Noah noticed that the trees behind Tank were still trembling, startling the butterflies off their branches.

Before he had time to wonder what else was headed their way, a line of white tigers came leaping over the rail, one of them crashing over the whiteboard. Within seconds, there were eight white tigers roaming inside the clearing. They paced around Tank, fangs exposed, heads rolling from side to side, tails snapping like whips. They were clearly on Tank's side, ready to protect him from the danger that had the big man in such a fright.

"I don't—" Richie stammered. "How did—"

"They crossed!" said Ella.

Noah nodded. Somewhere in the exhibit was a gateway to the Secret Zoo. Was it a straight drop? Or did it lead to the Grottoes—whatever they were. Noah glanced through the trees but saw nothing unusual.

Tank leaned on Tameron's shoulder, battling to catch his breath. After some time, he forced himself to stand straight.

"A sasquatch," said Tank, "we spotted one . . . in Koala Kastle. We lost sight of it . . . then we found it again. It attacked . . . got away."

Noah realized that Tank's injury had come from the razorlike claw of a sasquatch. He was reminded of the sasquatch that had tried to drown him only weeks before. With perfect clarity he recalled the cold water, the strength of the sasquatch's grip, the hatred in the beast's yellow eyes.

Growling, the tigers continued to pace around Tank.

"Tameron," Tank went on, "we need you back. We need to regroup and call . . . call our strongest forces. We've got to hunt it down."

"The other Descenders," said Tameron, "do they know?"

Unable to speak, Tank nodded. He leaned on his knees and stared at the ground, grimacing in pain. The white tigers continued to circle him, growling and shifting their weight. Then he turned to Tameron so quickly that a few dots of blood speckled the white fur of a passing tiger. "We've got to go," he managed to say. Then he and the tigers jumped the railing and vanished into the trees.

Tameron faced the scouts. His eyes were glassy and vacant, focused on an empty spot between Richie and Megan. It was as if his eyes had lost their purpose—as if fear had stripped him of his sight. Tameron was afraid, deathly afraid. Noah wondered how bad a sign that was. Without a word, the Descender turned and sprinted down the path Tank and the tigers had taken.

The scouts simply stood in silence, watching the branches settle. This was their first day of crosstraining, and already they were in the thick of things—the thick of something they could only begin to comprehend.

"Let's get out of here," Ella said.

"Totally," Richie agreed.

The scouts headed out. As they left the clearing, Noah studied the path that Tank and Tameron had followed. He couldn't see much, but he noticed the faint paw prints that the tigers had left in the dirt.

Paw prints that could be easily followed.

❧ CHAPTER 15 ☙

THE GROTTOES

"Megan!" Noah called out as he stood by the front door. "I'm going over to Richie's! I'll be back by supper!"

From somewhere inside the Nowicki house came Megan's response: "We just got home from school!" It was Wednesday, the day after the incredible incident at Butterfly Nets.

"Yeah . . . so?"

A pause, then Megan's voice. "Whatever. See you later."

Noah tore out the front door and grabbed his bicycle from the garage. At the street, he turned in the opposite direction. He had no intention of visiting his friend—he was headed for Butterfly Nets for a better look at the Secret Zoo passage that Tank and Tameron had taken. His parents wouldn't be getting home from work for more than an hour, so he had enough time to do this.

He sped down the street, swerving past kids who were still walking home from school. He turned onto the sidewalk beside Walkers Boulevard and soon pulled into the parking lot of the Clarksville Zoo. He left his bike and headed inside, waving his zoo membership card like a badge to the attendant at the booth.

He hurried across the zoo and slipped into Butterfly Nets, which was no longer "closed for construction." He walked beside the waterfalls and trees, and beneath the gabled glass roof. Butterflies darted all around. He smiled at an elderly couple, then crossed the narrow bridge to the clearing where Tameron had held crosstraining.

He stood at the railing along the edge of the open space and peered through the trees until he spotted the tigers' faint paw prints. The markings faded away toward the back of a tall rock formation. Noah moved around for a better angle to see behind the rock, but couldn't find one.

He could think of only one way to get a full look.

Noah glanced over both shoulders. The elderly couple

had wandered off and now had their backs to him. He took a deep breath and considered his next move.

"Don't do this," he told himself. "Just go home."

After glancing around a second time, he closed out his thoughts, then slipped through the horizontal bars. He hunkered low and stepped softly forward, twisting his body to avoid branches.

Somewhere, a door creaked. Noah stopped and peered out through the bushes and trees. Not far off, a family of five had just entered the building. Three young kids were jumping around excitedly, pointing at butterflies. They were headed down the visitor path in Noah's general direction.

A wave of panic washed over Noah. He hunkered lower than ever and hurried on. He reached the rock formation, which sat several feet away from an outside wall. The rock reached into the glassy heights, a waterfall splashing noisily down its front side. Butterflies were perched along it, warming in the sunlight. On the ground in the near-private space between the rock and the wall, a flight of stairs led into the dark earth. Here, the paw prints ended. Were the Grottoes at the end of the stairs? More than a dozen butterflies flew out of the dark ground and scattered into the air.

Somewhere in the exhibit, one of the children shrieked excitedly. Fear jolted Noah. He shouldn't be doing this.

Tameron had warned against entering the Grottoes. He'd said the scouts could get hurt, lost, or worse.

But Noah needed to learn the full truth about the Secret Zoo. From the Descenders to the Grottoes, too much was being kept secret. If everyone Noah cared about was in danger, he needed to fully understand what they were dealing with.

He shut off his thoughts and took a single step down. Then another, and another. The cool air sank into his flesh and a musty odor filled his head. He traded the light of the exhibit for the darkness of the underground. At the bottom of the stairs, a gloomy opening was at his right. It was perhaps six feet tall and four feet across. Noah peered into the opening but couldn't see much. But when he stepped into the corridor, it suddenly illuminated. In the walls, a few light bulbs were set; Noah's movements must have triggered them to go on.

Wide-eyed, Noah stared around. The short tunnel headed straight for ten feet and then stopped at two branches, one left and one right. He walked down and stared into both branches. Each was perhaps fifty feet long, and each had five or six new branches—mouths to new tunnels. All the entrances were covered with velvet curtains.

The Grottoes. Did the tunnels go to the Secret Zoo or somewhere else?

He took two cautious steps down the left branch. Old bricks formed the walls and arched ceiling. As he walked, he swept his fingertips along the wall. The bricks touched him back with their damp coolness. Flecks of mortar broke away and peppered the ground.

His thoughts rose like a voice in his head: *Get out. Down here . . . it's too dangerous. Tameron . . . he told you so.*

But was it possible that the Descenders were trying to keep something from the scouts? Could it be that the Grottoes weren't dangerous at all, and the Secret Society just wanted Noah and his friends to stay out of them?

Above the mouths of the new branches were thin metal plates with words engraved upon them. From where he stood, Noah couldn't quite read them. Did the letters spell out the places the tunnels led to?

For a better look, Noah walked on. But before he could reach the first tunnel, he halted. A cloud of something had burst through a distant branch; inside it, colors churned. Noah peered closely and realized what the cloud consisted of. Butterflies. Hundreds of them. Packed tightly together, they were pouring into the tunnel and streaming toward him.

Noah didn't have time to react. Almost at once the butterflies swarmed around him. Their soft wing tips brushed his skin, and Noah became engulfed in their movement. He turned back. Blinded by butterflies, he walked with his arms stretched out in front of him, feeling his way for the short passage that led to the stairs.

He thought again of Tameron. The Descender had warned him to stay out of the Grottoes. Was Noah about to pay a price for ignoring him?

He shook his arms in front of his face, batting away butterflies. It didn't help; he still couldn't see a thing. Panic filled him, and Noah blindly ran forward, sweeping his hand along the wall, feeling for his way out. Had he already passed it? He worried he might slip into the wrong tunnel and end up in some other place—a bad place, like the Dark Lands.

His hand suddenly dove off the bricks and floated in space. A passage. Noah turned to it but saw nothing through the stream of butterflies. He did his best to close out his fear and stepped forward. After only a few steps, the butterflies disappeared around him, and he saw the staircase that he'd climbed down. He glanced back: the butterfly swarm was stretching across the two branches that he'd originally seen.

He didn't know where the butterflies were going, and he didn't care. He just wanted to be out of the Grottoes. He hurried up the steps and stared out from behind the rock. The elderly couple was nowhere in sight. He hurried through the trees and slipped through the railing back into the clearing. He gasped. The family of five was standing with their backs to him at the opposite edge of the open space. Noah had forgotten about them.

One of the children swung around. The boy was no more than four years old, and his lips were encrusted in dry chocolate. He smiled broadly and pointed at Noah. "Look, Mommy!" he said.

The mother turned and her face opened with surprise. She touched her fingertips to her lips, then tugged on her husband's sleeve. "Uhhh . . . Dale?"

The father faced Noah and took a step back, wide-eyed with shock. "Oh my gosh! What happened to you?"

Noah stood there, unsure what was wrong. "Huh?"

"How did . . ." The father's voice trailed off and he pointed to Noah—his torso, his legs, his feet.

Noah scanned his body and almost fainted by what he saw. Butterflies were clinging to every inch of him. He wore them like clothes.

He felt his cheeks flush. "I . . . I don't know," he managed to say. He began to sweep his hands across his stomach and chest, as if dusting off dirt after a headfirst slide. Butterflies flitted into the air.

The parents stared on, slack jawed. Before they could ask another question—perhaps about who he was—Noah turned and ran, brushing butterflies off his clothes as he went. At the exit, he slammed through the door and fled across the landscape of the increasingly peculiar and mystifying zoo.

CHAPTER 16

WIDE WALT

The next day the scouts had lunch at their usual spot on a long bench in the school cafeteria. As normal, all students had checked their manners at the door. Kids squealed and laughed and crunched potato chips. Crumbs spread like dust. The day's meal consisted of a rubbery slip of meat, a mound of clumpy mashed potatoes, and a choice of vegetable: string beans or half-cooked corn, the latter being the popular choice, as it supplied ammunition for the catapults the kids made out of their plastic sporks. None of the scouts cared about eating. Richie rummaged through his meal, digging with his spork for something to inspire his appetite.

As the scouts quietly discussed the incident at Butterfly Nets, three kids approached their table: Walter White and his two cronies, Dave and Doug. Walt's reputation was legendary. He was regarded as the meanest kid not only at Clarksville Elementary but in the entire district. Where most bullies were tall, Walt was wide—startlingly so. His shoulders projected out twice as far as a normal kid's, making his head seem puny in comparison. When he walked, he swung his immense shoulders. Over his five years at Clarksville Elementary, those shoulders had swaggered past countless students, earning him the nickname Wide Walt.

The scouts fell silent. Experience had taught them that it was best to deal with Walt by pretending invisibility. Eyeing the scouts, Walt jerked a thumb in their direction and said to his buddies, "Check it out—the Action Dorks."

On cue, his cronies started to snort and snicker. Doug tossed a string bean that bounced off Richie's head and slipped through the small opening of his milk carton. Dave and Doug high-fived at the accomplishment.

The scouts said nothing, prompting Wide Walt to remark, "That's what I thought." This was Walt's tagline, and few of his conversations ended without it. Most days, Wide Walt could be heard roaming the halls, terrorizing students while parroting, "That's what I thought. . . . That's what I thought." Sometimes Noah wondered if Walt was less interested in picking on kids than in convincing others that his minuscule head was, indeed, capable of thought.

Walt ambled away, swinging his shoulders. Nodding at the crowd, his goons marched behind him, each holding a lunch tray pinched between a thumb and a finger, a display of strength for all to behold.

"Oh—real nice," Richie commented as he peered into his milk carton. "Just great. Now I have a . . ." His voice trailed off as he searched the cloud of his disbelief for the right words. "A stupid string bean in my milk."

Ella slid her milk carton across the table. "Here. You can have mine."

Richie pushed it back. "I don't want yours." He stared into the milky waters of his carton—a tiny lake where a green canoe floated. "I want mine, only with no string bean."

Just then, someone sitting at the far end of the table started to shriek. It was Joey Reiser, the smallest, weakest kid in the history of fourth grade. Wide Walt was stuffing mashed potatoes down the front of Joey's shirt. Noah looked around. There wasn't a lunch attendant in sight. No surprise: Walt knew how to pick his moments.

Walt scooped up another handful of mashed potatoes—this time from the plate of a fifth grader sitting
nearby—and stuffed it down the back of Joey's shirt.
Walt's cronies laughed their approval.

"Why is this guy such an idiot?" Megan grumbled.

Ella said, "He's mad because his head's the size of a
raisin."

"Should we do something?" Megan asked.

"Yeah," said Richie as he stared at his plate. "Pretend
we don't see anything. I don't need Walt coming back
to fill *my* shirt with today's menu. I'm in no mood to
spend the day with mashed potatoes cooling in my belly
button."

Noah heard himself say, "Walt! Why don't you get a
life!" before he could stop.

Walt swung his meaty face in the direction of the
insult. He locked eyes with Noah. With the better
part of his arm still buried in Joey's shirt, he muttered,
"What . . . did . . . you . . . say?" leaving a pause between
each word for effect.

All across the cafeteria, heads spun. Students gasped,
and sporks dropped from shaky fingertips. No one could
believe it—someone had just stood up to Wide Walt.

"Uhhh . . . Noah?" Richie whimpered. "You might want
to rethink your strategy here."

Maybe Richie was right. No one in his right mind

challenged Wide Walt. Noah turned away and stared at his tray.

Walt smirked. Then he grunted and said, "That's what I thought."

Hearing Walt's tagline filled Noah with rage. He pushed himself up from the bench. He'd been through too much lately to back away from a fifth grade bully. In the past few weeks, Noah had battled sasquatches, flown on the back of a penguin, ridden on a polar bear, slept in an igloo, outrun hundreds of lunatic monkeys, and ventured alone into forbidden territory in a secret kingdom. Compared to all this, Wide Walt was nothing.

Noah strode down the length of the table and stood directly before Walt, who still had his hand in Joey's shirt. Quietly, he said, "I'd love to pop that pimple you call a head."

Walt's face went pale with shock. Absolute silence claimed the cafeteria.

Behind him, Noah heard Richie whisper to Megan and Ella, "Well, girls. Today's the day we die, I guess."

An adult voice rang out. "Boys!"

Standing at the cafeteria entrance was Mr. Kershen, the mustached gym teacher. Seeing him, Walt lifted his arm from Joey's shirt and struck his best I'm-not-doing-nothing pose.

Mr. Kershen took one look at Joey's potato-covered collar and yelled, "White! What in the world's going on here?" He quickly assessed the situation. "Get down to the principal's office—now!"

Wide Walt groaned. As he trudged past Noah, he sneered, "You're going to pay for this, dork. Oh, you're going to pay."

Noah slid his foot out, tripping Walt. The biggest bully in the school stumbled forward, arms flailing. He crashed into an empty chair and banged against the table. A carton of chocolate milk spilled down his pants.

"White!" Mr. Kershen yelled. "Quit clowning around and get going!"

His face red with rage and embarrassment, Wide Walt headed across the cafeteria, his hulking shoulders slumped.

The cafeteria kept silent. All eyes were on Noah, who walked back down the long bench and dropped into his seat.

Ella leaned across the table and whispered, "That was totally, totally, and totally the most awesome thing I've ever seen in my life!"

Noah slurped his milk and glanced at his friends. The other scouts sat there in silent awe, still entranced by the first act of rebellion against Wide Walter White.

Ella grinned and went on, "Noah—don't you get how

incredible that was? You almost toppled the Great Tower of Walt."

Noah couldn't restrain a smile. "Yeah, well, he's no bigger than a sasquatch."

Richie said, "But he smells just as bad."

Together, the scouts laughed. At one end of the cafeteria, Mr. Kershen was dragging the bully to the principal's office. It may have seemed to some that the confrontation was over, but Noah was smarter than that.

The confrontation had just begun.

❧ CHAPTER 17 ☙

An Instant Marlo

Later that day at recess, while the other kids were dangling upside down from jungle gyms and spinning at dangerous speeds on the merry-go-round, the scouts sat in a quiet corner of the schoolyard discussing the Wide Walt incident. Just as Richie wondered when their next crosstraining might be, a tiny bright blue bird shot down from the sky and settled on Noah's shoulder. Marlo.

"Marlo?" said Megan. "What . . . what are you doing here?"

Marlo cast his eyes in all directions, surveying the playground to make sure he hadn't been spotted. Noah glanced around as well. The kingfisher was too small to be seen by anyone more than a few feet away.

Marlo opened his beak and let a folded slip of paper tumble into Noah's lap. A note. Chirping, the kingfisher shot his gaze at Noah, then at the paper. Noah scooped it up and unfolded it.

"Is it from Mr. Darby?" Megan asked.

Noah nodded, his eyes locked on the page.

"Read it," urged Ella.

"Now?"

"Yeah, why not? No one can hear you."

Noah considered. He glanced back over each shoulder—no one was near. Very softly, he read the letter:

> *My Dear Scouts,*
>
> *Tank would like to resume your crosstraining next week. Let us know if Monday after school is possible. We will only need ninety minutes. Send your answer on this letter back with Marlo. If you can come, please report to the Wotter Park exhibit at 3:45. And kindly bring a change of clothes.*
>
> *With warm regards,*
> *Mr. Darby*

◦ ◦ ◦

"That's it?" Richie asked.

"Yeah." Noah stared at his friends. Still on Noah's shoulder, Marlo ruffled his feathers. "You guys think our parents will be cool with Monday?"

The three scouts nodded.

"Okay." Noah reached out and slipped his fingers into Richie's open jacket, snatching a pencil from his friend's pocket of nerd gear.

Ella said, "It's sort of nice having a human convenience store following you around all day, isn't it?"

Smiling, Noah scribbled, WE'LL BE THERE and signed the note. He folded the paper and held it up to Marlo, who used his beak to pluck it from Noah's grasp like a minnow from shallow waters. Then the kingfisher sprang off Noah's shoulder and zipped across the playground—over the monkey bars, through the jungle gym, and out of sight.

"Not a bad way to communicate," Ella mused as she stared across the Marlo-less sky. "Kind of like an Instant Message."

"Yeah," Megan joked, "an Instant Marlo."

Noah steered the conversation back to the matter at hand. "Looks like we have a second crosstraining coming up."

The four of them shared a grave look.

Richie said, "The Wotter Park. A change of clothes. Why do I have this feeling we're going to be getting wet?"

With that, the school bell rang, calling them back to class.

❧ CHAPTER 18 ❧

THE WOTTER PARK

When the school bell sounded at 3:30 on Monday, the scouts used the bathrooms to change into their ridiculous uniforms and then headed for the zoo, their backpacks slung over their shoulders. They walked down Jenkins Street and took a side entrance into the zoo.

A cold wind swept across the landscape. Within five minutes, they reached the Wotter Park, a square, windowless building standing over twenty feet high. Though a sign marked the exhibit CLOSED FOR CONSTRUCTION!, the scouts knew better. After glancing over their shoulders to ensure no one was around, Noah used his magic key to unlock the entrance, and the four of them slipped through the big double doors.

The Wotter Park's main attraction was a glass aquarium. About half the size of a tennis court, it had high walls but no ceiling. It contained an island that was separated from the aquarium's glass walls by a channel of water. The island had steep hills with smooth slides for the otters to play upon. The slides emptied into a winding pool with a few tunnels that led to the outer channel of water.

"It's hot in here," Richie said.

"Totally," Ella agreed.

The scouts dropped their backpacks to the floor and stripped off their gloves. Caps soon followed, except for Richie's—he kept his on. They took off their jackets, revealing their embarrassingly ugly Clarksville Zoo uniforms. Noah glanced at Megan. The pointy tips of her oversized collar touched beyond her shoulders, and her stitched-on name tag screamed MEGAN in the curviest cursive font Noah had ever seen.

Ella said, "We're being punished with these shirts, right? I mean, I don't see any other reason."

"Are you saying you're not going to wear yours for school pictures?" Megan teased.

"They're not so bad," Richie argued. He buried his

whole hand in his chest pocket. "I could fit a lot of cool stuff in here."

"Richie," said Ella, "you could put a *toaster* in there."

They stepped forward and peered through the glass walls of the aquarium. Otters swam and played in the channel of water between the island and the glass. The scouts gasped and stepped back as someone suddenly appeared in the water, a girl with short blond hair and red bangs. Hannah. She swam underwater from around the corner, otters swerving around her. She was chewing a piece of gum. Noah had the crazy thought that she might blow an underwater bubble and pop it against her lips. When she drew near the scouts, she casually tipped her head.

The scouts simply stood there as inches away from them, Hannah swam. Incredibly, the Descender was wearing her long purple boots with the thick soles. She kicked past the scouts and swam into the turn at the opposite end of the aquarium, disappearing behind the island.

Silence. None of the scouts moved. Finally, Richie cleared his throat and said, "Funny-looking otter, huh?"

From the back of the aquarium came a loud splash. Hannah appeared again, this time on the island. She rose over the hills like a giant. With her purple boots and wet, multicolored hair, she looked like a monster on a bad movie set. Noah almost expected her to growl, snatch an otter, and bite off its furry head. Instead, she walked to the front of the island, stepping over the otters and water slides. When she was near the scouts, she jumped across the channel of water, pulled her waist up on the aquarium wall, and flipped over the glass in an impressive arc before landing gracefully on her feet. She propped her hands on her hips and stood facing the scouts, casually chomping her gum.

"Wow!" Richie gasped. "That was . . . that was really, really athletic."

Ella rolled her eyes.

"Ummm—hi," said Noah.

Hannah said nothing. She simply stood there in her dripping clothes. She popped another bubble. Her stare swept over the scouts, momentarily stopping on each name tag. Still smacking her gum, she said, "Nice shirts." She turned away and walked along the aquarium wall. "Follow me."

As the scouts clambered behind Hannah, Richie asked, "Aren't you cold?"

"A little bit." Noah guessed that she would have responded the same way if icicles were dangling from her skin. "You're going to be cold in a few minutes, too," she added.

"Great," said Richie. "Can't wait."

Hannah stopped, turned to the scouts, and leaned her shoulder against the aquarium in a casual, cool way. "First things first. You're not going to get a long history lesson from me, and I'm certainly not going to bore myself by talking about our role in protecting animals. I'm going to show you guys how to cross the Secret Wotter Park, and that's it. We got ninety minutes before your mommies put dinner on the table. That gives us enough time to get you into the City of Species and back."

Hannah blew a bubble, popped it, then licked the sticky film off her lips. Then she continued, "Few quick things about the Wotter Park. It has a straight drop to the Secret Zoo. Once you cross into the Secret Wotter Park, there are four city gateways—entrances into the City of Species." She popped another bubble. "Sector Thirty-one, the Secret Wotter Park, is more than a bit unusual. It's the result of a consolidation project."

"Consolidation project?" Megan asked.

"Yeah. The Secret Society needed to free up some space for a new sector, so we—"

"What was the new sector?" Megan asked.

"The Cemetery Sector."

"Oh," said Richie. "One of the"—he drew quotation marks in the air with his fingers—"*Forbidden Five.*"

"Look," Hannah told him, "that's not important. All you need to know is that the Secret Society moved the original Secret Wotter Park to a water tower, an existing structure in the City of Species. These days, most people call this water tower the *Wotter* Tower." She spelled it out. "*W-o-t-t-e-r.*"

Noah said, "So the Secret Wotter Park—the sector that we're about to gate into—it's actually inside a water tower in the City of Species?"

Hannah answered with a nod and a *pop!*

"How high?"

"High. More than a thousand feet."

Richie clutched the sides of his head.

Hannah continued, "One nice thing about the Secret Wotter Park is that it's pretty small, allowing Crossers quick access to the City of Species. The record for crossing Sector Thirty-one is two minutes and twelve seconds."

"Who holds it?" Noah asked.

Hannah tapped her chest.

The scouts didn't say anything. They stared at the teenage girl, still trying to figure her out.

"One bad thing about this sector is that crossing it means you're going to get wet." She paused, then added, "If you guys learn only one thing in crosstraining, learn this: the secret to getting quickly across any sector is being able to use the unique abilities of the animals that live in that sector. You need to *become* the animals."

Noah asked, "But how—"

"Follow me," said Hannah. "Follow me, and I'll show you."

With that, she turned and led the scouts around the corner of the aquarium.

ᕦ CHAPTER 19 ᕤ

THE SCOUTS GET WET

On the side farthest from the entrance to the exhibit, a door stood in the wall across from the aquarium. Hannah told them it was kept locked and instructed Noah to use his magical key. The room inside was narrow and had steps built into one wall. Hannah and the scouts climbed up the steps and entered a passageway in the ceiling of the exhibit. They crossed over the visitors' walkway, opened a hatch, and jumped down to the island in the middle of the aquarium.

Hannah led them to the pool on the island, into which all the water slides emptied. The scouts followed her, stepping over rocks and puddles. Curious otters romped at their feet, scuttling through their legs and stepping on their toes. Hannah crouched like a baseball catcher and gestured toward the bubbling water. "Down there," she said. "Right in the middle—that's the entrance to the Secret Wotter Park."

The scouts leaned over and struggled to see into the depths. Otters plummeted down the slides and splashed headfirst into the pool. Some squirmed back onto shore, their slender bodies sleek and slippery. Others disappeared in the tunnels that opened into the channel of water along the aquarium walls.

"What do we do?" Noah asked.

"You jump in," Hannah replied. "You should have plenty of air."

"Should?" Richie echoed.

Hannah smirked and popped her bubble gum. "First timers. Always so nervous."

"You said it's a straight drop, right?" Megan asked.

Hannah nodded.

"As opposed to the Grottoes," Noah said, fishing for information.

Hannah kept silent, dodging Noah's remark.

"I'll go," Megan volunteered. She flung herself forward feetfirst and sank, the churning water closing above her head.

Still smiling, Hannah shook her head. "That chick—it's no wonder she found the Secret Zoo."

Inspired by Megan, Ella jumped forward and splashed down. Like her friend, she immediately disappeared into the bubbling water, leaving no trace.

Noah corralled his courage and fell forward. The cold water stole his breath. As his body sank, the only thing he could hear was the muted gurgle of the water. His clothes filled with weight and clung to his body.

He opened his eyes. The walls were smooth and sloped like those of an inground pool. He noticed the tunnels that punched through the island to the outer channel of water. Above him, the choppy water sparkled as it absorbed the incoming light. Beyond the flickering crests, he could make out the shifting silhouettes of Hannah and Richie peering into the pool.

Noah realized he was softly being pulled toward the bottom of the pool. He looked down, expecting to find an otter tugging on his pants. Instead, he saw that his feet were being sucked into a narrow cavern. Water swirled around the cavern's mouth the way it does around a bathtub drain. As Noah sank, his body began to spin around—once, twice, three times. His legs were swallowed, then his waist, his chest, his neck. Finally, he was pulled completely into the hole, and the light of the world blinked out.

Consumed in darkness, Noah continued to spin. Once again he was in a tunnel descending toward the Secret Zoo. This time, however, he was making the trip as a Crosser, a real member of the Secret Society. He began to envision what the Secret Wotter Park might look like—this magical place inside a water tower high above a city of unimaginable wonder.

❧ CHAPTER 20 ❧

BREAK ON THROUGH
TO THE OTTER SIDE

In the tunnel, something cold and smooth dragged across all sides of Noah. He knew what it had been: velvet charged with magic. Noah had just gated into Sector 31 of the Secret Zoo, the Secret Wotter Park.

The tunnel came to an abrupt end. On a gush of water, Noah shot into a bright open space surrounded by steep mountainsides. His arms and legs fanned the air as he dropped fifteen feet and splashed into a huge pool of water. He swam to the surface through the blinding trail of bubbles his splashdown had created and emerged gasping for air.

"Here!" a voice called out.

He swung his head around. Perhaps twenty yards away, Ella and Megan were clinging to otters—two for each girl, one tucked under each arm. Another pair bumped against him. He draped his arms over their backs and allowed himself to be carried toward his friends.

The scouts had been deposited in the middle of a round lake, roughly two hundred yards across. The lake butted against steep, rocky mountainsides. It was as if the scouts had landed in the bowl of a volcano filled with water rather than lava. Great trees covered the cliffs and reached across the water, sunlight streaming through their branches. Ropes of ivy draped down. Waterfalls dropped from the hidden heights, spilling over rocks and raising clouds of mist.

Smooth channels were etched into the granite parts of the mountainsides. Filled with cascading water, they acted as waterslides. Hundreds of otters were cruising down the well-worn paths and splashing into the lake.

Otters scrambled over the branches and one another. In the water, more than thirty swam up to the scouts and began to circle them, their long bodies snaking around.

Noah looked up and spied the watery tunnel from which he and the other scouts had spouted. It resided in the hollow of a huge branch. Richie suddenly shot out, tumbled gracelessly through the air, struck the water headfirst, and promptly sank.

Ella said, "Is it too late to pretend we don't know him?"

Richie's head emerged, then bobbed like a buoy with a red cap. Miraculously, he'd managed not to lose his glasses. He slapped his arms around, splashing water everywhere. An otter bumped noses with him, then unapologetically kicked off against his chest.

"Richie!" Ella called. "Over here!"

He dog-paddled toward the sound of Ella's voice, not covering much ground—or water—for his efforts. Seeing this, two otters squeezed under his arms and quickly carried him over.

"You okay?" Ella asked.

Richie was coughing too much to answer.

Concerned, Ella leaned toward him. "Richie?"

His coughing subsided. "I think . . . I think I swallowed an otter."

Ella swatted his head, sending his pom-pom into a dance.

Just then, Hannah shot out through the hollow in the tree. With a diver's grace, she twirled and flipped and pierced the water, leaving not a ripple. Seconds later, she emerged in front of the scouts. She swept her red bangs off her forehead and asked, "What do you think? Piece of cake?"

"Maybe later," Richie said. "I just ate an otter."

More and more otters were swimming around them

now, wriggling and looping from spot to spot, only their backs and heads visible above the water.

"I don't see the gateways into the City of Species," Noah said.

"That's because you're not looking in the right spot," said Hannah.

Noah pointed to the rising cliff walls and said, "If we need to climb *those* to get out of here, it's going to take a lot more than ten minutes."

"Again, you're not looking in the right spot. Remember— you're in a tower."

Noah pondered for a moment and realized what he'd forgotten. The water. He squirmed off his otters and dove down into the lake. What he saw through the clear water was so breathtaking that he had to surface for air.

"What's down there?" Megan asked.

Noah took three shallow breaths and gasped, "No words . . . just look!"

With that, he sank a second time. The scouts—even Richie—swam after him. Just below the water surface on each side of them, a distant light blinked above a velvet curtain: the four gateways into the City of Species. The tower walls, made of glass, slowly curved inward, con- verging on a point no less than five hundred feet below. Through the distant glass floor, Noah saw gleaming col- umns and realized the tower had two parts: a round tank above a series of columns. With no visible seams or sup-porting framework, the walls offered an endless view into the City of Species. Noah saw buildings and trees and the faint suggestions of animals navigating the winding streets.

Almost bursting from lack of air, the scouts resurfaced.

"Unbelievable!" Richie spluttered, spraying water from his lips. "The walls! The glass! The city! It's . . . *incredible!*"

"But how . . ." Megan looked up around her. "All these mountainsides—what are they standing on? I mean, if everything beneath us is glass, how—"

"Don't smoke your brain thinking about it," said Hannah. "I'm not a magical scientist, so I couldn't explain."

"A what?" Noah asked. "A magical scientist?"

Hannah popped her gum. "You guys have so much to learn—but not from me, because, remember, I don't do the book stuff. Right now, the only thing I care about is getting you guys into the City of Species and back to the Clarksville Zoo. You ready?"

On behalf of the scouts, Noah nodded.

"Good. This next part makes gating into the sector feel like a walk in the park."

Richie said, "You're kidding, right?"

Hannah winked. "Get ready to lose your stomach."

❧ CHAPTER 21 ❧

ACROSS THE WOTTER TOWER

Each of the scouts once again clung to a pair of otters to stay afloat. More than a hundred otters were swimming around them, bumping heads and rumps while leaving V-shaped ripples in their wakes. The animals seemed to be anxious about something.

To be heard above the splashes and squeaks, Hannah loudly said, "Okay, as you guys saw, there are four city gateways equally spaced around the Wotter Tower. Each gateway opens to a different street in the city. We're going to take"—Hannah pointed her finger—"that one." She paused, chomped her gum, then said, "Ready?"

The scouts nodded.

"Just do like I do."

She waved her arm above her head, as if flagging down a taxi, and about twenty otters quickly closed in around her. She sucked back a deep breath and plunged down. As she started swimming, the otters packed in around her and began kicking their legs and undulating their streamlined bodies, propelling themselves forward. Though their movements were at first sloppy and unco-ordinated, they quickly synchronized. From the snout of the first otter to the rump of the last, waves rolled across them as if they were a single unit, causing Hannah to be carried away.

Just when Noah wondered how Hannah would breathe, her otters rose to the surface in a smooth arc, allowing her to take a breath before plunging her back down, their pointy tails whipping the air.

"I'm going," said Megan without hesitation.

"Cool," Richie said. He pushed his glasses back up the slippery slope of his nose and added, "On your way back, let me know how it went."

Following Hannah's lead, Megan waved her arm in the air, alerting the otters. Then she dove into the water and began swimming toward the gateway. Quickly, a pack of otters dipped down and squeezed into place along her body. They began to kick and undulate, first individually, then as a unit. Finding their rhythm, they carried Megan forward.

"I'll go," Ella volunteered next. "Before these river rats start munching on my fingertips, which started looking like prunes about five minutes ago."

She waved her arm and dove down, where a pack of otters quickly gathered around her. Within seconds, Ella was being carried across the tower.

"Okay," said Noah. "My turn." He drew in a breath and plunged in. Sound left his world. He held open his eyes to watch the otters move in around him. He was pulled, poked, and pressed as the animals jostled for position. When they took off swimming, Noah was pummeled by their hard noggins and wide rumps. But soon their movements harmonized and the otters took control of Noah like a strange underwater puppet. He discovered what it was like to swim with an otter's grace, speed, and flexibility.

After a few seconds, the otters brought Noah toward the surface so abruptly that his stomach dropped. They surfaced long enough for Noah to take a breath and then dipped back into the water.

They gained speed. Noah peered out over his shoulder: across the underwater reaches of the Wotter Tower, hundreds of otters were playfully chasing him.

Seconds later, the otters again lifted him to the surface

for air. Noah saw the mountain was less than thirty yards away. Its closeness meant the city gateway was close as well.

The otters dipped Noah back down into the water. Soon the world darkened as they swam beneath the mountainside. Noah could make out a shadowy ceiling of rocks and roots. Somehow the mountain stood on nothing. Noah suspected it clung to the glass walls of the Wotter Tower the way mud clings to a brick wall. The details of the gold curtain came into view: the long vertical folds, the dangling tassels, the gold loops holding the curtain to its rod.

Noah could see far across the City of Species—its buildings, trees, and streets. It seemed to be waiting for him. The distant animals looked like toy figures spread across a toy city.

Panic swept over him. The gateway was hundreds of feet high. How would he get safely down? Just as he had this thought—a thought he should have had all along—the otters released him and veered off, narrowly avoiding the wall.

A second before Noah struck the gateway, he threw his arms up to shield his face. He wasn't afraid of the curtain—he was afraid of the fall that waited just beyond it. As Noah soared into the incredible heights above the City of Species, he screamed.

❧ CHAPTER 22 ☙

ABOVE THE CITY OF SPECIES

Noah's arms flailed as he tried to grab onto something. A thousand feet beneath him, the city streets waited. Everything took on a dreamlike quality. He suddenly wondered if this entire adventure was just a product of his restless mind. From Marlo's first tap-tap-tapping visit at Noah's window to the march across the Dark Lands to Mr. Darby's invitation for the scouts to join the Secret Society to Noah's current freefall from a water tower as high as the clouds—all of it now seemed a part of a long, vivid dream.

Something thwacked against his head and jolted his

thoughts. His body touched down into something wet.

He glanced around. He was lying on his stomach in a narrow stream of water, like those in the granite channels of the Secret Wotter Park. But out here the water was simply streaming through the air. Totally bewildered, Noah peered back over his shoulder. He saw the velvet curtain, which was draped across an opening in the massive glass wall. Water gushed along the edges of the curtain and shot into the air, but instead of dropping, it simply hovered there, a rushing river suspended in space.

As Noah continued to stare behind him, something crawled up his back. He was nose to nose with an otter. The animal was stretched out, riding Noah like a sled. Apparently it hadn't let go of him inside the Wotter Tower. The otter shot Noah a worried look and then peered in both directions, brushing its stiff whiskers across Noah's cheek.

Just as Noah was about to crash into the building across from the Wotter Tower, the right side of his body swept upward, and he veered in a new direction. He soared beside the wall, his body horizontal again. Around him, the rushing water bubbled and churned.

Noah realized that he was on a glass slide. To make certain, he stroked his hand along the invisible wall, which arched up and over his head. The slide was fully enclosed—a glass tunnel in the air. He peered into the depths of the city and spotted the slide's trail of bubbling water spiraling down.

The slide turned sharply left again, sweeping Noah and the water along. Noah had completed a full turn and was now headed back to the Wotter Tower. The velvet curtain, already fifty feet above him, burst open, releasing a pack of otters and a gush of water. The animals wrestled and rolled over one another. For them, being a thousand feet above the city was ordinary stuff.

As Noah came within ten feet of the Wotter Tower, the slide veered sharply to the right. Again Noah rose up the smooth curve. Water splashed all around as the slide straightened to run directly beside the wall. Noah saw his image reflected in the glass. Lying on his stomach with his arms stretched out in front of him, he looked like a flying superhero wearing an otter for a cape.

The slide passed the Wotter Tower, then flew by a building framed with trees. It curved around columns and balconies, and arched over roofs and branches, sometimes so suddenly that Noah's stomach dropped inside him. He began to make out the details of the animals below: the spots on giraffes, the slashes across zebras, the ears on elephants.

Noah veered sharply right and began to cross the street. He punched into the thick foliage of a tree and his world exploded with color and movement. Leaves were escaping the summer-long clutches of their branches, piling on the slide's roof and spilling over its sides. They partially covered the glass, revealing its full shape—a perfect spiral, about six feet wide.

The slide pushed through the far side of the tree, and Noah saw that he and the otter were less than three hundred feet from the ground. The not-so-distant animals continued to rise into focus. Noah saw tails wagging, manes blowing, and feathers swaying. He saw two teenagers on a bull, a woman on a tiger, and a group of kids in a huge basket strapped to an elephant. Across the city, he spotted the Library of the Secret Society and its massive staircase.

The slide went on and on. As it neared the ground, its slope began to decrease. At ten feet high, it had completely leveled out, like the final stretch of a playground slide. Noah and the otter began to slow as they glided beside the heads of taller animals. Just ahead, their ride came to an end at a large fountain in the middle of a busy intersection. Water spilled over the fountain's chest-high walls into a trench along its perimeter.

Noah and the otter dropped through the air and splashed down. Once they'd slowed to a stop, the otter pushed off Noah's back, and Noah stood up. He staggered to the edge of the fountain, threw his arms over the wall, and collapsed. The otter swam up and waggled onto the ledge. It stood on its hindquarters in the steady overflow of water and gazed at Noah.

"Enjoy the ride?" Noah asked.

The otter tipped its head to one side, as if contemplating its answer. Then it sniffed the air toward Noah, the point of its snout wriggling.

Hannah was standing nearby, dripping water onto the street. Near her, two ornate marble benches faced each other. On one sat Ella and Megan, both soaking wet. On the other sat two adults, both perfectly dry. One adult had a gleaming bald head, the other a long gray ponytail. Tank and Mr. Darby.

With a grunt, Noah heaved his body over the fountain wall. He landed in a watery trench and splashed across it, frightening a group of pelicans into the air. He staggered to the benches, his wet, spongy shoes leaving puddle footprints in the street. The otter chased after him, its paws leaving watery prints as well. Noah stared at his sister, whose wet pigtails clung to her head.

Megan said, "Tell me—was that cool, or *what*?"

"Right now, I'm leaning toward *what*."

Noah dropped onto the bench beside Tank, who was bellowing with laughter.

"C'mon!" Megan protested. "You can't tell me that wasn't totally cool!"

Noah kept quiet. He kicked off his shoes, pouring

water onto the street. Then he leaned forward, his elbows against his knees. Directly in front of him sat Ella. She'd taken off her shoes, too, and was wringing out her socks. Noah had a sudden bird's-eye view of her bare feet. He was shocked to see that her toenails were painted pink.

"You paint your toenails? Since when?"

Ella twisted her wet sock, grimacing with the effort. "We just came down a waterslide the size of the Empire State Building, and you want to talk about my toes?" She studied Noah's face and saw that he was serious. She shook out her sock and said, "I don't know. A few months ago, I guess."

Noah looked over at Tank, who was still staring at him with a broad smile.

"Now that's what I'm talking about!" said Tank. He held a triumphant fist out to Noah. "Give me one of these!"

Noah simply stared at the massive ball of Tank's fist. Each knuckle was the size of a walnut and marred with a web of scars, as if Tank had spent a lifetime punching holes in glass.

"Huh?" Noah mumbled.

Tank wriggled his fist in the air. "One of *these*. C'mon, now. . . ."

When Noah directed his confusion to Mr. Darby, the

old man said, "Mr. Pangbourne would like you to raise your fist and touch it to his. It's a variation of the conventional handshake, and I believe it demonstrates a heightened level of respect or admiration toward another person." Mr. Darby glanced at Tank and asked, "Is this assessment correct, Mr. Pangbourne?"

"As always, Mr. D."

Noah thought about this for a second and then lightly punched his small fist against Tank's huge one. The gesture felt a little awkward, but exciting at the same time. Tank threw back his head and laughed again. Noah realized for the first time since sitting next to the big man that a thick bandage covered the far side of his face.

"Tank—your face—"

"What about it?" Tank said with a wink. "You noticing for the first time it's not so pretty?"

Noah opened his mouth, but no words formed.

"The bandages?" Tank said. "Yeah, that sasquatch got me pretty good. I took enough stitches to sew a pair of pants, but I'll live."

Mr. Darby pointed upward and said, "Here comes our last scout now—not so courageously, I'm afraid."

Noah stared overhead. Barreling toward them in the glass slide was Richie, scarcely visible in a knot of more than a dozen otters. He was hurtling forward with his knees pressed to his chest and his rear end aimed at the sky. His screams echoed out of the tunnel and over the fountain.

With no emotion or surprise in her voice, Ella said, "Here comes Richie," and continued to wring out her socks.

❦ CHAPTER 23 ❧

THE OCEAN IN THE SKY

Richie and the otters splashed down in the fountain, scattering birds into the air. Gasping, he staggered over to the fountain wall and threw himself against the ledge. The otters swam in all directions, their eyes bulging with fear. Before they fled the area, a few nipped angrily at Richie. He labored over the wall and stood there, swaying and dripping.

"What happened?" Noah said. "There were so many otters—what did you do?"

"I'm not sure," said Richie at last. His glasses hung sideways on his face, perched closer to his ear than his nose.

"The curtain . . . the otters . . . I just . . . I just sort of blacked out."

Mr. Darby and Tank threw back their heads and laughed.

Richie walked over and took a seat beside Ella. Realizing that his glasses were crooked, he fumbled to correct them. "This place is going to kill me, I swear."

"It was a slide," said Megan. "We figured those out in kindergarten, remember?"

"Hmmm . . ." Richie muttered. "I don't seem to remember the ones that *rose through the stratosphere*."

"Nicely done," Mr. Darby said. "All of you." He leaned toward the scouts and became serious. "I came to check on your progress and to let you know that we are still on the hunt for the sasquatches since the attack on Tank. We have, in fact, stepped up our efforts. We've been scouring the sectors day and night."

"Have you found anything?"

Mr. Darby shook his head. "I'm afraid not."

"What will happen if you don't find them?" Ella asked.

"Impossible to know," Mr. Darby answered. "For now, keep focused on your task—developing as Crossers. Leave the sasquatches to our concern. You can take comfort in knowing our strongest forces are on the case."

"Strongest forces?" Noah asked.

"Yes," Mr. Darby said. "The animals and . . ." His voice

trailed out and he briefly shifted his stare to Tank. "And others."

"What do you—"

The old man stood, clapped his hands together sharply, and said, "Now, then! Mr. Pangbourne, I do believe we have other business to attend to."

Tank rose from his seat. "That's a fact, Mr. D."

Megan protested. "But we just got here. . . ."

"And you have only thirty minutes to get *out* of here." Mr. Darby tipped his head to the scouts. "*Ta-ta,* my young scouts. I leave you in the quite competent care of Hannah." The two men walked into the street, quickly disappearing into the hordes of animals.

Noah's gaze shifted to the otter who had ridden his back and was now sitting on the bench beside him. The otter stared up and twitched his whiskers.

"You still here?" Noah asked.

The otter blinked twice.

To the scouts, Hannah said, "Okay, let's go. You heard Darby—we've got to get you back."

The scouts squeezed into their wet shoes and followed Hannah into the street.

"Ugh," Ella said as she pulled the cling out of her wet zoo shirt. "I can't wait to be dry again."

"Get used to it," Hannah said. "It goes with the territory. You'll be back in dry clothes soon enough."

The otter ambled beside Noah, swinging his head from side to side, taking in the teeming city. Noah asked Hannah, "Any chance you know the name of this one?"

"That's Louie," Hannah said. "He has a way of making trouble."

Noah stared down at the otter. "Hey, Louie."

Again returning Noah's gaze, the otter snorted and shook the water from his hindquarters.

Hannah and the scouts merged into the busy crowd on the street, finding a spot between a family of grizzly bears and a bunch of emus. One of the emus pecked at Richie's pom-pom as if it were a snack, prompting him to escape to a new spot beside Hannah. Noah stared overhead and tried to locate the waterslide. Though he couldn't see the glass, he saw a slender stream of water rushing through the shower of autumn leaves.

A quick stroll returned them to the Wotter Tower. The scouts followed Hannah into the shadowy space beneath the enormous tank, where streets ran, animals roamed, and fountains spouted. More than two hundred feet above him, the bottom of the tank bulged out like an overturned dome. The massive reach of the water made it seem as though an ocean had emptied into the sky. Movements in the water caused shimmering beams of sunlight to fall across everything.

"Hannah," said Noah, "all this water—where does it go?"

"All over the City of Species—pools, fountains, slides, streams."

"Where does it come from?"

"Mostly the water exhibits in the Clarksville Zoo. The rest . . . well . . . we sort of borrow it from the plumbing on the Outside."

The scouts chuckled at the idea. The Secret Zoo, despite its magic and power, got some of its water through ordinary plumbing.

Hannah led them to one of the many marble columns that supported the tank. At its base, a velvet curtain hung over an open doorway—a gateway back to the Secret Wotter Park. Hannah pushed through the curtain and led the scouts into a small, damp-smelling room. Louie trampled across their feet, settled into a spot, and made a strange otter sound, a cross between a squeak and a grunt.

Hannah's voice rose in the darkness. "Brace yourselves."

As the curtain settled back into place, the entire room jolted upward. The scouts were in some type of elevator, and in the hollow darkness of the marble column it had begun to climb. Noah felt the elevator's speed in his shaky feet.

In seconds, a bright light filled the room as they emerged from the marble column into the circular tank.

The elevator, made of glass, was rising along the inside curve of the tower wall, pushing through the water. One side had a view onto the City of Species, while the other sides looked into the Wotter Tower. Noah stared down through the bubbly trail of the elevator's wake and saw the streets miniaturizing again.

Noah realized a wall of water stretched across the place where the curtain once hung. Somehow the water wasn't spilling in.

Hannah said, "Go ahead. Touch it."

Noah stepped forward. The water made no sound as droplets splashed against him. He raised his arm and punctured the water with a finger. He felt its rush against his skin. He spread his fingers and pushed his arm forward, allowing his hand to be devoured. Then he swiveled his wrist, investigating the sensation of the pressure.

Hannah said, "The curtain that normally hangs there leaves traces of its magic. Our scientists found a way to use that magic to keep the water back."

As Noah pulled out his hand, the water closed around his fingertips. He stepped away to allow Megan and Ella a turn, and joined Richie in staring into the City of Species. Rooftops spread out around them: glass domes, bamboo thatch, and gabled sheets of steel. Freestanding columns rose into the heights. Birds of all sizes and species sailed through the crowded sky. A sprawling mesh of branches formed elevated streets for mobs of arboreal animals to cross.

Noah noticed six vertical tracks between the tower wall and the elevator. Gears spun across them. This was what was lifting the elevator.

As they soared into the upper part of the tower, the water filled with otters. They swam in all directions, rolling and somersaulting and playfully biting one another. At least fifty otters spotted the elevator and rushed over to race it. They swam upward, exposing their white bellies and leaving V-shaped ripples in their wake.

Louie charged to the open wall and dove out to join his friends.

Ella said, "I vote that next time we skip the slide and take the elevator."

"It's a one-way ride," Hannah said. "Bottom to top, one stop. Unless you can time it just right on its way back down."

They suddenly broke through the surface of the water, and a tangle of tree limbs came into view. As the elevator followed the curve of the wall, it began to pull back into one of the Wotter Park's mountainsides. From their vantage point, the rocky walls seemed to be extending in front of them. The walls soon closed on themselves somewhere in front of the elevator, and the world around the scouts turned pitch-black.

"Oh nice," Richie said as the elevator continued to stream upward. "Glad this isn't freaky or anything."

The elevator stopped with a jolt. The scouts couldn't see a thing.

"Reach forward," Hannah said.

Noah did. A velvet curtain was settled across the open wall of the elevator again.

"Now follow me."

Noah felt Hannah brush by as she slipped through the curtain.

Megan said, "Time to go home," and went next.

Ella followed. Then Richie, though not without complaint. Noah was the last to go—the last to leave the Secret Zoo behind.

CHAPTER 24

BACK INTO THE WOTTER PARK

On the other side of the curtain was a wall of water like the one they'd touched in the elevator. After stepping into it, Noah saw a point of light a few feet above his head. He swam to it and arrived in a small, underwater cavern with smooth concrete walls. He realized he was somewhere inside the fabricated island in the Wotter Park exhibit. To one side was an opening. Noah swam through it and emerged in the channel of water beside the aquarium walls, his friends in front of him.

Following Hannah's lead, the scouts hoisted themselves onto the island. The Descender led them out of the exhibit, following their path of entry in reverse: through a hatch in the ceiling, then down the steps to the door that opened into the visitor area. They stepped into the walkway, their wet sneakers leaving tracks.

Hannah indicated their backpacks on the floor. "Dry clothes?"

The scouts nodded.

Hannah's eyes passed over them and she said, "You guys all right? You don't look so good."

Standing with his arms crossed over his body and his hands clutching his elbows, Richie shivered. "I'm freezing!"

Hannah continued to look them over. Her bangs clung to her forehead, her clothes to her body. She worked the gum between her jaws, chewing slowly and deliberately. For a moment—nothing more than a few seconds—her stare softened. She seemed to feel something for the scouts.

"I know you're cold," she said. "So am I. Crossing is tough. It's a huge responsibility, and it's not for the weak." She seemed to consider something and then added, "Think about the places you're going to be required to protect. As a Crosser, you're going to need to know the ins and outs of our entire world—and I mean that *literally*."

She paused and waited for the scouts to say something. When they didn't, she began to speak again, her thoughts and words coming more rapidly.

"It took magic to create our world—a magic that's still alive and all around. Every day the Secret Society struggles to contain it, to understand it, to use it. Think about its power. Look at the City of Species. Crossers are ready to die to keep that power from DeGraff."

The scouts quietly listened.

"I know that the Secret Society does important work—great work—but there are times when . . ." Her voice trailed off and her gaze fell to the floor. Just when it seemed she'd forgotten her thought, she finished it: "There are times when many of us wish our world had never been created. Our civilization . . . it was born from madness and magic. Where does that put us?

"The four of you can walk away. You're not bound to this place—you're not bound by our burden."

She became quiet, leaving a strange, empty space in the conversation that Noah dared to enter.

"What divides your world from ours?" he asked. "Nothing—a thin layer of dirt." He paused, searched for the right words, and found them. "In facing your problems, we only face our own."

Behind him, the scouts nodded.

The Descender shifted uneasily. She popped a bubble, turned, and walked off. At the door to the room with the built-in steps, she stopped and swung around. "Look, you have to understand something. We can't permit you to fail. If you fail, *we* fail—all of us—and we've worked too hard for that to happen."

Understanding this, the scouts nodded again.

"You kids are from the Outside. Outsiders are weak. And where there's weakness, there's danger." She paused. "But Darby sees something in you, that's for sure. And I admit that old man has a good eye for stuff—and for people, too."

She left another awkward silence—a silence that Noah filled with a question he'd been wanting to ask for a long time.

"Hannah?"

"Yeah?"

"Those boots"— he pointed to her feet—"you're always wearing them, and they're . . . they're just so strange."

Hannah's stare moved across the four scouts. She breathed out a small pink bubble that burst against her lips. With a quick lap of her tongue, she wiped her mouth clean. "They're just boots. I wear them 'cause I like them."

She turned and climbed the steps. The scouts heard her footsteps across the ceiling, then they watched her fall from the hatch onto the island. She glanced at the scouts and casually dropped into the pool to the gateway that would take her home.

"They're *not* just boots," Noah said. "Hannah's not

telling us everything. The Descenders—they're hiding something from us."

Megan nodded. "Yeah, I get the same feeling."

The scouts said nothing else. They grabbed their backpacks, rummaged inside for dry clothes, changed in the exhibit's bathrooms, then stepped out of the Wotter Park into the early darkness.

As they walked across the cold zoo landscape, their eyes scanned the dark surroundings for signs of movement— signs of the Shadowist. They kept quiet, their thoughts turned to the mounting strangeness and mystery of the Secret Zoo.

CHAPTER 25

WORDS FROM A DICTIONARY

After their adventure at the Wotter Park, life went back to normal for the scouts for a week. In school they tried to focus on their work and steer clear of Wide Walt, who was surely planning some type of retribution for the cafeteria incident. At home they spent the evenings hanging out in Fort Scout, their conversations about the Secret Zoo and their next crosstraining. They wondered about the Descenders, worried about the sasquatches, and guessed about the Grottoes. Thanksgiving came and went.

On their walk home from school on Monday, the last

day of November, the scouts were delivered another Instant Marlo when the kingfisher flew out of nowhere and perched on Noah's shoulder. The note asked if the scouts were available to crosstrain on Saturday morning at nine o'clock. The scouts sent the note back with a "yes" response, then made plans for a Friday night sleepover at the Nowickis, which was rarely a problem with their parents. Ella often stayed with Megan, and Richie with Noah. On Saturday, the scouts could wake early and head to the zoo together.

Now, it was almost midnight on Friday night. Noah and Megan's parents had retired to bed. The scouts were lounging around in their pajamas in the living room. Ella and Megan sat on the couch, Noah lay on the floor, and Richie sat all the way back in a large, pillowy recliner. In whispers, they were talking about the Secret Zoo.

No one understood the butterflies Noah had seen in the Grottoes. Where exactly had they come from? Where did they go? And why were there so many tunnels? Did they all go to the Secret Zoo? If not, then where?

They thought about the Descenders. What had moved inside Tameron's backpack? Why did Sam have zippers on his jacket beneath his arms? Why did Hannah have such strange boots? And why did the four teenagers resent the scouts so much?

At one point Richie struggled out of the deep cushions on his recliner and said, "Bathroom break. I'll be back."

He left the room, then reappeared a few minutes later. As he strolled across the carpet, Ella said, "Honestly, Richie—those pajamas . . ."

Richie stopped and looked at his outfit. His shirt and pants were covered with miniature R2-D2s.

"What's the matter? You got something against droids?"

Ella smiled. "If we look up *dork* in the dictionary, I'm pretty sure we'll find your class picture."

Richie happened to be near a bookcase when Ella said this. He scanned the books and then pulled out a thick dictionary. "Let's just see about that." He thumbed through a few pages, touched his finger to a place, and said, "Nope. No Richie." Then he flipped forward a bunch of pages. "But if we go here . . . Ah, yes. Here's my picture. Under *genius*."

The scouts laughed.

"Look up *descender*," Noah said.

"Huh?"

"Just look it up. Is it even a real word?"

Richie turned to a page, read a few lines, then set the weighty dictionary on the floor beside Noah. "Weird," he said. "Check it out."

The scouts huddled around and read from the page.

de·scend·er *noun* 1: in printing, the part of a lowercase letter that extends below the body; for example, in the letter *y*, the descender is the tail, or that portion of the diagonal line which lies below the *v* created by the two converging lines.

"Doesn't make much sense to me," Ella said. "We're talking people, not letters."

"Agreed," said Richie.

Noah lifted the dictionary up to Richie, who planted it back into the row of books.

Around one o'clock in the morning, they decided to go upstairs to bed. As the girls slipped into Megan's room, the boys went into Noah's. Richie immediately fell asleep, but Noah didn't. He lay in bed, fitfully tossing and turning. He couldn't stop thinking about what had happened to him in the Grottoes.

An hour passed. Then another. Noah's bedside clock showed the time in glowing digits: 3:10. Noah finally dozed off and then woke, groggy and worried. The clock read 7:57. He angrily threw off the covers and went downstairs. He poured a bowl of cereal. Halfway through it, he became curious about the word *descender* again. What they'd read in the dictionary hadn't made sense—not when applied to people.

A thought filled his head. He stopped crunching on the cereal and sat perfectly still, a bead of milk streaming down his chin.

Maybe the scouts had focused on the wrong word.

He jumped from the table and went to the bookcase in the living room. He pulled out the dictionary, sat on the couch, and starting flipping through the pages. Instead of stopping on the word *descender*, he stopped on the word *descend*. Then he read from the page.

> de·scend *verb* 1: to approach or pounce upon, especially in a greedy or hasty manner 2: to attack, especially with violence and suddenness 3: to sink or come down from a certain intellectual, moral, or social standard.

Noah tapped the page and stared off into space. He thumbed forward and found the word *descender* again. Once more, he read the definitions.

"These don't mean anything," he said to himself. "They don't . . ."

He fell silent. A few of the words in the definition seemed to jump off the page. He read out loud the phrases that struck him as important: "'The part . . . that extends below the body . . . the descender is the tail . . . created by the two converging lines.'"

He raised his eyes and stared at the wall.

"'The part below the body . . . the tail.'"

The definition undoubtedly referred to letters. But was it possible that the Secret Society was using it to refer to something else? Noah scanned the passage again.

"Like an animal's tail?" he asked himself.

He focused on the final words, *created by the two converging lines,* and remembered his first day of crosstraining, and how Tameron had mentioned that there were two lines of defense protecting the sector gateways, a line of humans and a line of animals. Each line had its own strengths.

What if these two lines of defense could converge? What if the two species that protected the Secret Zoo could become one? With the intelligence of a human and the strength of an animal . . .

Noah scoured his thoughts for something meaningful, something relevant. Four distinct images came to him: Tameron's backpack; Hannah's long, bulky boots; the zippers and buckles on Sam's jacket; and the pin-size holes in Solana's leather outfit.

His heart began to hammer. He focused his gaze back on the dictionary. As he tried to locate *descender* on the page, he stumbled across another word: *descendant.* Could being a Descender have something to do with being a descendant?

No, Noah told himself. "Descender" *and* "descendant" . . . *two different things.*

But weren't nicknames suggestive rather than literal?

But a descendant of what? he asked himself. He thought of the short history of the Secret Zoo—not more than a hundred years. What kind of ancestry could this blip in time include?

Forget it, he told himself. He slammed the dictionary closed. *You're overtired—making something out of nothing. Try to relax.*

But there was no way he was going to relax. Not now. Not until he had some answers about who the Descenders really were. Not until he understood the Grottoes and their purpose.

Noah checked the clock: 8:10. The scouts planned to leave for crosstraining around 8:45, before Noah's parents normally woke. Maybe he could get to the zoo early and have another look at the Grottoes. This time he'd be more careful. This time he'd run down the tunnels, read the engraving on the plates, and then get out. He could leave a note with his friends telling them that he'd gone early to the zoo.

Without another thought, he went upstairs and quietly got dressed in his bedroom, stepping over Richie in his sleeping bag as he walked between his dressers. Back downstairs, he put on his jacket and red cap and slipped into the garage. He grabbed his bike and silently stepped out the side door.

He pedaled down the street, his thoughts on the Grottoes. At Walkers Boulevard, he turned right. As the Clarksville Zoo appeared in the dim morning light, Noah realized that in his haste he'd forgotten to leave his friends the note.

✿ CHAPTER 26 ✿

BACK TO THE GROTTOES

Noah parked his bike and headed to the zoo entrance. The attendant at the front booth was a bit surprised to see Noah so early in the morning, but she simply waved at him as he spun the turnstile. Being a Crosser came with its privileges, Noah thought, and one of those privileges was not being questioned by zoo workers about early morning visits.

He ran across the zoo grounds. The shortest path to Butterfly Nets involved cutting across a series of connected paths—concrete to dirt to concrete again. All across the zoo, animals raised their heads at the commotion. Realizing that he was making too much noise, Noah slowed to a jog.

As he passed the outdoor exhibits, he peered into them. They prickled with activity. At the Bear with Us! exhibit, a pack of watchful black bears prowled a concrete mountainside. At Ostrich Island, a crowd of ostriches jostled for space, their blocky, feathered rumps colliding. At the Elephant Event, several elephants roamed the yard, their trunks swinging, their ears flapping, and their ivory tusks stabbing up at the yawning sky.

Noah reached Butterfly Nets and used his magic key to get inside. The exhibit was quiet and still. He hurried across the bridge to the clearing, slipped through the rails, and headed to where the Grottoes waited. When he reached the stairs, he stopped to stare down into the darkness.

Just be careful, he told himself. *Read the engravings, then get the heck out.*

He took one step, then another, then began to breathe in the cool air of the Grottoes. At the bottom of the staircase, the lights switched on. He walked down the short passage to the two branches—one left, one right—and looked in each direction. The Grottoes were perfectly still. He peered out at the distant metal plates but, as before, he couldn't read them from his angle.

He took a step down the left branch and fear halted

him. He remembered the butterflies and the blinding way they had flown all around him, causing him to lose his bearings.

He peered at the plate above the nearest tunnel. He could faintly see the engraving, but he couldn't yet read the letters.

Be brave, Noah told himself. *And be quick.*

He took five fast steps, stopping at the mouth of the first tunnel. Above the curtain, an engraving read, THE SECRET ELEPHANT EVENT. He moved to the next tunnel, which read THE POLAR POOL. Then he went to the third tunnel, which read THE SECRET KOALA KASTLE.

He realized something. The name above the second tunnel was different than the other two. It was marked THE POLAR POOL rather than THE SECRET POLAR POOL. Why? Why was the word *secret* missing? Why had—

His thoughts stopped. He heard something beyond the mouth of the fourth tunnel. Stomping. Something was headed for the gateway—a large animal. The tunnel floor trembled. Flecks of mortar skipped down the brick walls.

The curtain suddenly burst inward, and a rhino plodded into the Grottoes. The curtain slid off its horned snout as the big animal turned in Noah's direction, pressing him against the wall. As the rhino rumbled down the tunnel, it swept against Noah, twisting and pulling him along.

A second rhino brushed the curtain aside. A third, a fourth—each one on the tail end of the one before it. They either didn't see Noah, or didn't care that he was there.

Noah sloppily stepped sideways, trying to prevent himself from twisting in a knot. His cheek scraped the brick wall and the front of his jacket tore open.

Several feet to his right, a curtain dangled. Noah had to get to it or risk being squashed. He squirmed several feet along the wall and then was pushed through the gateway. Water engulfed him and Noah understood why: he'd passed through a wall of water similar to those in the Wotter Tower elevator.

It was pitch-black. His legs kicking, Noah twisted and turned. He lost his sense of direction and couldn't decide where the curtain was. When he tried to rise for air, he bumped his head. He swam back and forth, sweeping his arms above him, hoping to find an opening or a place to surface. Nothing.

In his panic, Noah quickly ran out of breath. His heart began to hammer painfully in his chest. He finally detected a sliver of light and swam to it with all his might. Just as he reached it, the world blinked out and the pain in Noah's chest stopped.

In the dark body of water connected to the Grottoes, Noah had passed out.

CHAPTER 27

THE SCOUTS WAKE UP

Richie was munching on a mouthful of sugary corn-flakes when Ella poked her head into the dining room.

"Where's Noah?" she asked.

Richie shrugged. "Haven't seen him." Milk dribbled down his chin. "He was already up when the alarm clock went off this morning."

It was just before 8:30. Noah and Megan's parents were still sleeping, and Ella, Megan, and Richie were dressed and almost ready to leave for crosstraining.

Ella went upstairs. Noah's bed was empty, and so was the bathroom. She headed back into the kitchen, where

Richie had just loaded another spoonful of cereal into his mouth.

"You haven't seen him all morning?"

"Nuh-uh," Richie struggled to say through a mouthful of food.

"And don't you find that a little strange?"

Richie stared into the corners of his eyes and considered this. Then he looked back at Ella. "Not until just now." He wiped milk off his chin with the back of his hand. "I thought maybe he was . . . you know . . . using the bathroom."

"For a half hour?"

Richie shrugged.

Megan stepped into the kitchen and shook her head. She'd been looking in the basement for her brother.

"Anyone check Fort Scout?" Richie asked. "Bet you anything he's out there."

Megan said, "I'll go." Then she rushed out the back door.

As Megan tore across the backyard, Ella squinted her eyes at Richie. "A half hour . . ."

Richie shrugged a second time. Then he lifted the cereal box toward his friend. "Hungry?"

❧ CHAPTER 28 ❧

TROOP 112 SPOTS A PAW

Shortly before the Clarksville Zoo opened at 8:30, the members of Troop 112 were lined up outside the main gates, rubbing their hands and rocking to stay warm. The troop consisted of five boys and a den leader, Mr. Davis.

When the gates opened, the troop barreled through a turnstile and headed for Arctic Town. They reached it within minutes, the six of them steering through the area's exhibits, which looked like sights near the North Pole.

They stopped at the Polar Pool. Icy-looking boulders and low rock formations lay scattered around a long, inground pool. Near the middle of this glacial plain sat the biggest rock formation, the size and general shape of a school bus. Just five feet in front of it was a long row of squarish boulders capped with fake snow and ice. In front of those stretched the winding pool. Between the large rock formation and row of boulders was a path, a favorite place for Blizzard and Frosty to stroll.

The Polar Pool's big attraction was an underwater glass tunnel that stretched across the width of the pool. Each end of the tunnel opened to a glass-walled room accessible from a flight of stairs.

The troop stepped onto a sidewalk surrounding the exhibit. One of the boys stood on the bottom rail of a low steel fence and stared across the fake icy tundra. "Hey! Where are the bears?"

The other kids stepped up beside him, bobbing their heads as they searched for a view around the boulders.

"Don't know," said a boy with buck teeth that were practically smaller than the braces cemented to them.

"I don't see any," said a boy with beady glasses.

"Look!" shouted a boy with orange freckles. "Over there, behind that row of boulders! A paw! See it?"

"Nuh-uh."

The boys began craning their necks in all directions for a better look.

Though the freckled boy had partly spotted one of the polar bears, he couldn't yet see what it was doing. The polar bear, having just dragged Noah out of the water, was licking his face, trying desperately to wake him.

❧ CHAPTER 29 ☙

Noah Gets Spotted

Noah opened his eyes and peered out at a world that was hazy and indistinct, as if a fog had rolled into his bedroom. For some reason, his mother was dragging a wet washcloth over his face. When he grunted and rolled away, she didn't stop. Angered, he struggled to focus his stare. Hovering above him was not his mother but a polar bear. What he thought was a washcloth was the bear's tongue. And Noah's bed wasn't his bed—it was the hard concrete of the Polar Pool exhibit.

He sat up with a jolt and coughed up water. A wave of pain sloshed across his head, and the world teetered and turned around him. He held his temples until the pain subsided and the earth steadied.

He stared up at the polar bear.

"Frosty?" Noah asked. Frosty was Blizzard's smaller, female companion.

The bear tipped her head to one side and growled gently.

Noah suddenly remembered what had happened in the Grottoes. He must have passed out in the water. Frosty had apparently discovered him and dragged him out. Now the day was bright, the sky cloudless and blue. Noah peeled back the sleeve of his jacket and read his waterproof watch: 8:37.

The zoo was open.

Noah glanced around. He was in the path between the big rock and the low wall of boulders. He peered out through one of the gaps and saw into the pool. The tunnel snaked through the water, each end opening into a glass room whose dim light kept the tunnel aglow. Beneath the rippling water, the tunnel seemed to swell and sway.

"Frosty . . ." he muttered. "You've got to get me out of here. Fast."

The polar bear pointed her muzzle at Noah and grunted softly.

Noah began to stand and stopped. Standing on the sidewalk along the exhibit were six people, five boys and a man. They were gazing into different areas near him. One of the boys—a kid with big orange freckles—stared straight into Noah's eyes.

Noah dropped out of sight again. He'd barely shown himself, and only for an instant, but he knew it had been enough.

Noah had been spotted.

❧ CHAPTER 30 ☙

THE BOY WITH BIG ORANGE FRECKLES

The boy with big orange freckles gasped. "What was that?"

A chubby boy glanced at him. "What was what, Cayden?"

"*That!*" The freckled boy, Cayden, jabbed a finger to where he'd seen the boy's head poke up. "Alex—you didn't see that? Someone's behind those rocks! A kid in a red hat."

The rest of the troop, including Mr. Davis, regarded Cayden with a bewildered stare. Across the Polar Pool exhibit lay a wall of rocks and a body of water. Nothing else.

"I'm dead serious! He was wearing a red hat—a poufy red hat."

"Maybe it was Santa Claus," one kid quipped. "Fell off his sled."

The troop erupted in laughter.

Ignoring the others, Cayden pushed away from the rail and hurried along the sidewalk, circling the Polar Pool exhibit. As he walked, he pointed into the exhibit, calling out, "Behind those rocks! C'mon—you'll be able to see better from over here!"

The rest of the troop stopped laughing. Mr. Davis stepped forward, saying, "Let's check it out, at least."

Together, the six of them followed their freckled friend. As the path between the boulders and the rock formation became visible, they stopped and stared out. About eighty feet across from them lay a polar bear, but no kid.

Alex said, "Well, if there was someone in that exhibit, that bear just ate him."

The troop broke into laughter again.

"I know I saw someone. . . ." Cayden's eyes widened as a fresh thought came to him. "Wait a minute—that kid— he's got to be on the other side of the bear!"

This brought forth the biggest laugh yet from the other boys.

Cayden swung around to them. "It's not funny! I'm telling you—"

"Hold on," said Mr. Davis. "The bear's starting to move. We'll know in a sec if there's a boy in there, or if our big white friend mistook him for breakfast."

The den leader's remarks prolonged the laughter. The only one who kept quiet was Cayden. He stared into the exhibit, watching the bear rise to her feet, certain that the boy he'd seen was about to be revealed.

⟢ CHAPTER 31 ⟣

A VIEW FROM FORT SCOUT

Megan dashed across the cold grass and climbed the ladder to the tree fort. She poked her head through the opening in the floor and peered around. Fort Scout was empty. She hoisted herself up and stared out at the bridges and lookout platforms. Nothing.

The zoo grabbed her attention. Could Noah be somewhere in there? All of his crazy interest in the Grottoes—did he do something stupid this morning?

She snatched up the binoculars and held them to the bridge of her nose. She slowly surveyed the zoo and saw nothing out of the ordinary: zebras lounging beneath trees, gazelles strolling across their yards. In the near side of the zoo, her stare stopped on an unusual dark spot along the stark white sprawl of boulders in the Polar Pool.

Megan gasped. It was Noah.

❧ CHAPTER 32 ☙

FROSTY STEPS ASIDE

The polar bear lumbered to her feet and turned to face the troop, her long neck swinging from side to side. The freckled boy stared anxiously, waiting for the animal to step out from the path. The other boys stopped laughing and fixed their eyes on the exhibit.

"Okay," Alex said. "We'll know in a second."

The polar bear stepped out from the boulders. Then she turned away from the troop and strolled toward the pool, leaving the path behind her exposed. Nothing was there.

Cayden's jaw dropped in disbelief. Another boy, thinking it would have been cool to find a kid trapped in a bear exhibit, groaned in disappointment.

"But . . . a kid . . ." Cayden stammered. "I saw a kid. . . ."

Mr. Davis laid his hand on the freckled boy's shoulder and said, "Don't worry about it. Sometimes our eyes play tricks on us—it just happens." He turned to the rest of the troop. "It looks like our bear's going for an early morning swim. You boys want to go down and watch from the tunnel?"

The boys nodded and headed back the way they'd come, toward the staircase that led into the ground. As they walked away, Cayden kept turning his head to stare at the low wall of boulders. He was still certain he'd seen a boy in a red hat.

CHAPTER 33

NOAH GETS STUCK

Noah could hardly believe he'd been able to wedge himself between two of the boulders. The gap was barely wide enough to roll a basketball through, yet he'd been able to squeeze his entire body into it. It had been a strain—his body pulling, twisting, tugging, and shifting—but it had worked. Now, even with Frosty out of the way, the boys couldn't see him from their vantage point.

Through the opening, Noah watched Frosty pad toward the pool. Very softly, he whispered, "C'mon, Frosty. Get me out of this mess."

Frosty splashed down. Water sprayed through the gap that Noah was wedged into, drenching him. He heard rapid-fire footsteps from his right. The boys were headed out, probably for the staircase that led to the underwater tunnel, which was to his left. Frosty was luring the boys away—but if Noah didn't get behind the wall of boulders again, they would see him as they passed by.

Noah tried to pull himself back and couldn't. He was wedged tight between the rocks, unable to move anything but his head and hands.

The boys' footfalls grew louder. They were getting close to an open view of Noah again.

Noah squirmed and twisted. He managed to plant the bottom halves of his legs on the ground in front of him. He hoped he could push against them and squeeze farther back behind the boulders. But when he tried, he didn't budge.

The footsteps drummed louder. One of the boys came into view. Then the others. If a single one of them glanced in his direction, Noah would be discovered.

Noah froze, his cheek pressed against a boulder. With wide eyes he stared out at the boys, and in a hushed whisper, chanted, "Please don't look . . . please don't look. . . ." Just as he became certain that one of the boys would glance in his direction, the last of them disappeared from view. Their footsteps faded into silence as they descended the underground staircase.

Noah breathed a sigh of relief, then immediately realized it was premature. He heard a voice. A man was talking—the guy that Noah had seen with the boys. He and someone else were headed up the path, trailing the others. Knowing that it was pointless to try to free himself, Noah kept perfectly still. Maybe, like the rest of their group, they wouldn't look.

Noah suddenly felt sick. He'd been a Crosser for only a few days, and already he'd failed—failed the Descenders, failed Mr. Darby, and worst of all, failed his friends. How had sneaking into the Grottoes ever seemed like a good idea? How had he been so stupid, so selfish?

The man's voice grew louder. Distinct syllables took shape. Within seconds, he and his companion would have a clear view of Noah.

A wall of white fur suddenly sprang up right in front of Noah. Frosty. She had pushed her paws against the pool's edge and hoisted herself. As she splashed back down, water exploded in all directions and gushed through the gap. The fresh wetness broke the seal that held Noah to the rocks, and he was able to tug and squirm his way out.

Noah hit the ground with a wet *thwack!* He rolled behind one of the boulders and curled up, holding his breath. He listened to the man and the boy walk past him, then tread down the stairs.

Letting out a slow breath, Noah muttered, "Nice one, Frosty." Sitting with his back to one of the boulders, he began to scan the ends of the exhibit, searching for an escape.

CHAPTER 34

OLD IRON AND PINKY PEDALS

Megan couldn't believe what her binoculars were now showing. In the Polar Pool exhibit, her brother had just squeezed out from a low wall of boulders after being splashed by a bear. Now he was skulking around, crouched low like an advancing soldier, jumping in and out of the cover of the fake rocks.

She leaned through the window for a better look, slowly turning the focus knob on the binoculars. "You've got to be kidding me. . . ."

Noah ran down the gradual slope of the perimeter trench. Twenty feet below the ground, he skirted the outside wall, dragging his fingertips along the concrete, hoping that his touch might reveal something—a secret exit, no doubt.

"C'mon, Noah," Megan whispered. "Get out of there!"

Noah jogged through the trench and disappeared from view on the other side of the exhibit. Megan jerked the binoculars around, hoping to find him. Inside the lenses, the magnified world jumped and whirled.

"C'mon . . . c'mon . . . c'mon. Where are you?"

Noah stepped into view again, this time over the gradual slope from a different part of the trench. Still hunched over, he steered through the big rocks, glancing all around. He was searching more recklessly now, looking lost and confused.

There's no way out, Megan thought. *He's trapped!*

Noah rounded a boulder too suddenly and accidentally stepped over the edge of the pool. He tumbled into the water, landing without a splash in the silent world of Megan's binoculars. A series of circular waves rolled out from the spot where Noah had disappeared. Her brother was gone. Just . . . *gone.*

"No!" Megan cried out.

Her heart pounding, she threw herself onto the slide and hit the ground running. She raced across the yard and banged through the back door too loudly. In the kitchen, Richie and Ella turned with a jerk.

"What's wrong?" Ella said.

"We got to go! We got to go *right now*!"

"Shhh," Ella said. "Don't wake your parents. What's going—"

"It's Noah!" Megan forced her voice down to a whisper. "He's trapped in the Polar Pool!"

Ella slapped her hands over her mouth and Richie stood from the table, his spoon plunging into his cereal bowl. Without another word, the scouts rushed into their jackets and hats and headed into the garage, Megan pressing the button to open the big door.

Megan said, "We'll take the bikes."

They rushed into the mess, finding Megan's bike but not Noah's.

"Noah took his," Megan said.

She grabbed her pink bike and shoved it toward Richie. "Here."

He stared at the bicycle but didn't take it.

"Pinky Pedals?" he said. Pinky Pedals was what Megan jokingly called her bike.

"Take it!"

Richie mounted the seat and eased his way onto the driveway.

Megan walked to one side of the garage and rolled out Noah's minibike. A stinky, wretched thing that had survived her father's childhood, it looked as if it had been constructed by mounting a seat and two wheels to a lawn mower engine wrapped in steel. The minibike had a name: Old Iron. Gas-guzzling and loud, it steered erratically and spewed foul smoke. But its top speed was thirty miles per hour, and it had room for two.

Megan turned to Ella. "Grab one of those helmets and hang on!"

Ella's eyes widened. She straightened her earmuffs, swung one leg over the bike, and took a seat behind her friend. "Oh boy," she uttered.

"Richie, follow us."

Megan hit the ignition switch—a button fastened to the rusty handlebars with plastic ties. The minibike grumbled and wheezed and spat out a massive cloud of oily smoke. She opened the throttle and roared off the driveway, out into the street.

CHAPTER 35

THE DEPTHS OF THE POLAR POOL

Noah's drenched clothes sank him ten feet under. Just in front of him was the glass tunnel. It ran across the pool, its curved roof five feet below the surface, its floor pressed flat against the ground. Through its glass, Noah saw the backs of the boys and the man. They were looking away from him, watching Frosty as she wrestled with an orange barrel in the water, putting on her best show to hold their attention.

The pool was long and narrow, perhaps twenty yards across and three times as long. The tunnel sat near its middle. In front of Noah, on the other side of the tunnel, the pool ran straight until it ended. Behind him, it ran straight and then doglegged right. If Noah tried to swim in either direction, he'd surely be spotted. The only way out was the way he'd entered—back up to the water's surface.

Frosty suddenly fixed her black eyes on Noah. She stopped wrestling the barrel and craned her long neck to peer around the boys at him, her rigid stare revealing her puzzlement.

The old man straightened as he realized Frosty was looking at something. Certain the man was going to turn and spot him, Noah swam to the bottom of the pool and melted into the shadows below the tunnel floor. Hidden from view, he gazed upward. The man stepped to the tunnel wall directly above him and stared out, his hands cupped around his eyes.

Noah waited . . . and waited. His lungs began to burn for air.

The man turned and rejoined the boys. Noah poked his head up. Everyone had their backs to him and their eyes on Frosty, who once again was distracting them.

Now was his chance. Inches from the tunnel wall, he swam to the surface, his arms and legs stroking madly as he struggled against his wet clothes. As he went, he was suddenly seized by his jacket collar and spun around. Objects that looked like white tree trunks were stroking the water on both sides of him. A polar bear was pulling him along. The bear's jaws were clamped onto his collar, and the force of the water had Noah pinned against the animal's stomach, making for a bumpy ride.

But if Frosty was playing with the barrel on the other side of the tunnel, who was this?

There was one answer: Blizzard. The mighty polar bear had emerged from somewhere—maybe a cavern in the big rock formation above, maybe the Secret Zoo—and, spotting trouble, had dived in to help.

The water around Noah began to brighten. Blizzard wasn't only swimming forward, he was also swimming up, and Noah understood why. The angle concealed Noah from view. If someone inside the tunnel were to look their way, they'd see nothing but the bear's wide back.

Blizzard rounded the bend at the far end of the pool, leaving the tunnel out of sight. There was no underwater view into this part, which stopped ten feet away at a concrete wall.

Blizzard broke through the surface and released Noah, who greedily sucked back a breath of air. Noah turned and bumped his nose on the bear's long muzzle. Blizzard's wet fur clung sleekly to the contours of his head.

Noah opened his mouth to say something, but was immediately pulled back into the water. The bear plummeted and headed straight for the end of the pool, where a small section of the wall swung inward. Blizzard swam with Noah through the opening and the hatch fell shut, triggering on a row of lights in an underwater tunnel. Bricks the size of shoe boxes lined the mossy walls. Patches of stringy seaweed swirled and swayed.

The Grottoes. A different area of them.

Perhaps forty yards long, the tunnel branched at least ten times. Velvet curtains were draped across the mouths of the branches. Before Noah had a chance to read where they went, Blizzard turned, paddled through a gateway, and emerged in the middle of another dark underwater cave. No longer than twenty feet, it was shaped in a curve. Beyond the opening at each end lay a bright channel of water bounded by a wall of ice and a wall of glass. Noah realized that they were in a rounded corner that connected two perpendicular channels of water.

Something crashed into Blizzard. A penguin. It veered wildly from the impact, banging against the cave wall. At least five more penguins steered around them, whapping them with their stiff flippers as they swam into the bright, adjoining channel of water.

Noah realized they were in the huge aquarium in Penguin Palace, the penguin exhibit in the Clarksville Zoo. This four-sided aquarium had a six-foot-deep channel of water that bordered a fabricated iceberg. It had glass walls with concrete corners; visitors could see through the walls, but they couldn't see into the corners.

More penguins closed in on Blizzard and Noah. The bear spun quickly, shoving his wide rear end out at them. A few penguins dodged to the floor, bumping Noah's feet as they passed. Others swerved to the sides. Blizzard swam with Noah out of the corner cave and emerged into the bright water. To their left now was the tall iceberg; to their right, the tall glass wall. As penguins continued to swim around them, Noah saw their feathered rumps and rising trails of bubbles.

Without slowing, Blizzard momentarily surfaced, allowing both himself and Noah a breath of air. As he dipped back down, he cut in front of a penguin. The bird dodged to the side, struck the glass wall, and slid across it, the curve of its bulbous belly pressed flat.

About halfway along the channel of water, Noah gazed through the aquarium wall and his heart dropped. Just beyond the long stretch of glass stood several people, visitors to the zoo.

Blizzard and Noah were being watched.

CHAPTER 36
THE BA-EH AND THE BA-OY

In the dim light of Penguin Palace stood a middle-aged woman. She was talking on her cell phone, pacing the room, and ignoring her two young girls, who were standing inches away from the big aquarium. One girl was two years old, the other five, and both had their palms pressed flat against the glass. The girls stared bright-eyed into the aquarium, watching a parade of penguins swimming below the surface, their bodies swooping up and down, leaving a wake of bubbles. Dim aquarium light spilled onto the girls' faces, softening their already delicate features.

The two-year-old raised her arms and clapped her palms against the glass. The resulting *smack!* resonated through the glass-and-concrete quarters of Penguin Palace.

"Penguin!" she said—or meant to say. But her inexperienced tongue got caught on the nub of her pacifier, causing the word to come out like "Pah-gwah!"

"That's right," the five-year-old said, touching her sister's shoulder. "Pen-guin," she repeated, careful to enunciate each syllable.

They smiled at each other. As they directed their attention back to the aquarium, the five-year-old gasped and took a step back. A polar bear, white and massive, was swimming toward them from around the corner, its thick legs paddling sluggishly. It nearly filled the channel between the glass and the iceberg, and, inconceivably, it was pulling a boy along, its jaws locked on his jacket collar. The boy seemed perfectly calm, as if this type of thing happened every day.

The five-year-old's chin dropped. Her wide eyes felt ready to burst from their sockets. Unable to move or even breathe, she watched the bear swim in front of her and then off toward the corner at the far end of the glass, penguins squirting around it. She had a plain view of the bear's short-tailed rump as it casually swam into the dark turn and disappeared.

For a few seconds, neither sister spoke. They simply stared into the corner after the bear.

It was the two-year-old who finally broke the silence. Around a mouthful of pacifier, she said, "Ba-eh. Ba-oy."

The five-year-old glanced back at her mother, who apparently hadn't seen a thing.

≼ CHAPTER 37 ≽

THE UNDERWATER HANDOFF

Blizzard swam around another dark corner and emerged on a different side of the aquarium. Noah felt a rush of relief when he saw that there were no people here. Blizzard hauled him up to the surface for a fresh breath.

Noah had no idea what Blizzard was trying to do. He was more worried than ever. Penguin Palace was seeing its first visitors of the day, and Blizzard and Noah were swimming around in plain view.

Halfway down this side of the aquarium, Noah's feet bumped against something. He looked down to see a penguin squeezing between Noah and the aquarium floor.

Its body bobbed with each stroke of its flippers, and it held the bear's speed. The penguin was so big that Noah recognized it immediately. Podgy.

Noah, his toes skipping off the penguin's feet, thought how surreal his circumstances had become: he was being pulled through a zoo aquarium, a polar bear above him and a penguin below.

Blizzard dropped Noah squarely on Podgy's back. The scout held on and allowed his legs to float out behind the penguin's feet. It was a familiar position for them, in the water as well as in the sky.

Blizzard swung around and headed back the way he'd come. Noah glanced over his shoulder and watched the bear's furry rump shrink as the two animals swam apart. As Blizzard disappeared into the dark corner, Noah was certain that the bear would swerve into a cave and escape Penguin Palace.

Podgy carried Noah into the final bend of the aquarium. As the light blinked out, they veered toward the iceberg and plunged into a hole. Noah had no guess where they might end up.

❧ CHAPTER 38 ❧

OLD IRON MAKES A FUSS

Megan sped Old Iron across the parking lot to the main entrance of the zoo. She realized that she couldn't waste the time required to get into Arctic Town—not the time it would take on foot, anyway. As she saw it, there was only one way to get across the zoo quickly enough. With this in mind, she steered the minibike onto the sidewalk, where at least twenty people were walking.

"Mooove!" Megan hollered.

Ella squeezed her friend's waist. "Are you nuts?"

People jumped off the sidewalk in all directions,

leaving a clear path. Megan raced forward at full throttle. Old Iron clipped a garbage can, knocking it aside with a hollow-sounding *clunk* that exploded crumpled napkins into the air. She rode through the open gates of the zoo, bounced onto the shortest path to Arctic Town, and sped away, no doubt leaving a lasting impression on the crowd. The people at the entrance would surely have the image of Megan burned into their heads for the next few months: her hard scowl, her snapping pigtails, her body leaning over the handlebars of the minibike—an unlikely machine of terror.

Megan glanced back and spotted Richie. He was steering Pinky Pedals through the people scattered all around, saying, "Excuse me . . . sorry . . . pardon me . . ." and continuously ringing the bell on the handlebars.

Deeper inside the zoo, people idled beside exhibits and struggled to stay warm, their hands pulled up into their sleeves and their chins buried in their jackets. As Megan rolled forward, Old Iron's growl raised curious glances: a young girl racing a battered minibike across the zoo was not an ordinary sight.

When they sped past the outdoor exhibits, the animals awoke, curious at the sound. Some craned their necks to watch her go; others ran along the edges of their yards. At Little Dogs of the Prairie, more than thirty prairie dogs jumped to their haunches for a better view. At the Strip of

Stripes, a dozen zebras stampeded across the grassy plain and raced along the fence beside the noisy minibike.

She suddenly became conscious of the time. How much had passed? How badly now did Noah need help? Frightened by the possible answers, she squeezed the throttle, and Old Iron hurtled forward at maximum speed.

Seconds later, she spotted something that made her hammer the brakes. Tires squealing, the minibike went into a slide and came to a stop. Richie pulled up beside them.

"No way," Ella said as the three scouts stared at the scene in front of them. "How?"

❧ CHAPTER 39 ❧

FLAMINGO FOUNTAIN

Noah rode Podgy through the underwater tunnel. Streaked with algae and slime, it had many branches, each one covered by a velvet curtain. Noah read the plates as they sped past: THE POLAR POOL; THE SECRET WOTTER PARK; A-LOTTA-HIPPOPOTAMI. Podgy abruptly veered into a tunnel marked FLAMINGO FOUNTAIN.

The new tunnel looked like the others Noah had seen, but longer. It continued straight for at least a hundred feet before ending at a point of light. Seeming to understand that Noah needed a breath, Podgy picked up speed. Pressure built against Noah's face, and the earflaps on his cap wagged like the ears of a sprinting dog.

They reached the end of the tunnel and emerged in a pool of water. This one was square and shallow. The big penguin leaped like a porpoise into the air so that Noah could breathe. As they splashed down, Noah fell off and tumbled, his arms and legs banging on the floor of the pool. When he stopped, he stood up in water that came to his chest. Sensing something beside him, he turned and saw a flamingo—a two-story-high statue of a pink flamingo standing on one leg. Noah was in Flamingo Fountain, the indoor fountain near the center of the Clarksville Zoo. This time, the Grottoes hadn't opened to an exhibit or a sector—this time they'd ended at an ordinary fountain.

Noah watched Podgy circle back through the water and disappear into the tunnel. Noah was on his own from this point on.

Flamingo Fountain was housed in a small glass building. Noah stared out through the clear wall in front of him and spotted three people: a boy on a pink bicycle and two girls on a smoky minibike. He couldn't believe it—the scouts!

Noah staggered to the edge of the fountain and climbed out. He stepped through the glass door and stumbled over to his friends.

"Noah?" Megan said.

"Megan?" Noah said. He pointed an unsteady finger at Old Iron. "That's . . . that's my minibike."

"Yeah, I know," said Megan. "We've got to get out of here. I think I just made a bunch of people really, really mad. And I don't want to hang around for questions."

Ella hopped off Old Iron. "Here," she said to Noah. "I'll follow you guys."

Noah climbed onto the minibike and clasped his arms around Megan's waist.

Megan turned to her friends and said, "Head to the back gates."

She squeezed the throttle, spun Old Iron around, and raced the battered minibike deeper into the zoo, Richie pedaling after her, and Ella following on foot.

CHAPTER 40

THE ESCAPE INTO GIRAFFIC JAM

As the scouts raced across the empty zoo toward the back gates, someone charged out from behind Giraffic Jam, a young teenager with a knit cap and a big backpack. Tameron. He stepped onto the sidewalk, waving his hands over his head. Megan squeezed the brakes and narrowly avoided hitting him. Ella and Richie stopped, too.

Tameron looked furious. He said, "Can't go that way. Cops are all over the exits."

"Cops?" Megan said. "The police are here?"

"I guess someone didn't appreciate you guys almost

running them over at the gates. People got cell phones, you know."

"Then where—"

"This way," Tameron said. "We need to hide you out. Follow me."

He led the scouts to Giraffic Jam, where two security guards ran up to them.

"Take the bikes," Tameron said. "Hide them."

The guards shot angry looks at the scouts, snatched away the bikes, then quickly rolled them off.

"Let's go," Tameron said.

The Descender led the scouts into Giraffic Jam. The circular building was twice the size of a movie theater. At least thirty feet overhead, ivy-covered walls ended at a domed ceiling made of glass and framed with narrow steel beams. Trees were scattered about, and waterfalls splashed into shallow beds.

In front of the scouts, a flight of steps rose to a wooden deck. More than ten feet off the ground, this deck circled the interior of the building, providing a place for visitors to feed the giraffes. The animals would stretch their necks over the railing of the walkway and use their long tongues to lap pellets from the visitors' palms.

"C'mon!" Tameron said.

He charged up the stairs and the scouts followed, their footfalls thumping on the planks. Sunlight pierced the domed roof and spread across their bodies. The Descender stopped at a spot along the railing and stared out. At least ten giraffes were idling around, chewing on leaves and grass. He waved his hand over his head and whistled loudly. A giraffe turned, spotted the Crossers, and swiftly walked over. It stretched its neck across the railing, lightly bumped its big head against Noah, and batted its long, plush eyelashes at the scouts.

"Do like I do," Tameron instructed.

He faced the giraffe and made a clicking sound with his tongue. The animal swung its neck across the walkway, nearly plowing over Megan. When the giraffe's neck came around to Tameron, he reached out and wrapped his arms around it. The giraffe hoisted him off the walkway and over the rail. Then, with a quick drop of its head, it lowered Tameron to the ground.

Other giraffes stepped forward, their hooves crunching fallen twigs. As they swung their heads over the walkway, the scouts wrapped their arms around their necks, allowing the animals to lift them over the rail and down to the grassy floor. Then they chased after Tameron, who was already making his way across Giraffic Jam.

Near the middle of the building, Tameron stopped and instructed the scouts to get behind him. He made the clicking sound again and called out the name of one of the giraffes, Lofty. The giraffe lumbered over to a thin waterfall and poked his head through it. They heard a groaning sound, like a lever being pulled, and immediately the hard earth in front of the scouts began to quake. Lofty plucked his head from the waterfall and gave it a shake, raining droplets all around. A rectangular piece of the ground, big enough to park a car on, broke free and started to rise. Steel poles were lifting it, one on each corner. When the section had risen about eight feet in the air, it halted, sending a thin shower of dirt and leaves over its edges. From one side of the new hole, a steep, dusty ramp disappeared into the darkness below.

Starting down the ramp, Tameron waved the scouts along, saying, "Let's go. You can hide in the Secret Zoo until the cops split."

The friends glanced at one another in hesitation. Then they followed Tameron down beneath Giraffic Jam.

☙ CHAPTER 41 ❧

THE CONFRONTATION

Beneath Giraffic Jam was a tunnel with four branches. The main passage was lined with ordinary bricks and was tall enough to accommodate the long necks of the giraffes. The opening to each branch was covered with a curtain, and metal plates above the curtains named the passages: METR-APE-OLIS, THE SECRET RHINORAMA, THE STRIP OF STRIPES, and THE SECRET GIRAFFIC JAM. Tameron hurried through the curtain leading to the Secret Giraffic Jam. As the scouts pushed through it, the curtain's tassels danced around their feet.

Inside the new tunnel, the ground inclined to a point

of light. The scouts quickly walked the distance and emerged into the sector, their feet moving from the hard earth to the wooden planks of a deck.

The Secret Giraffic Jam was a gigantic version of the Clarksville Zoo's giraffe exhibit. Noah remembered Tameron explaining how a sector, during its creation, took on the characteristics of the exhibit connected to it. This seemed especially true of the Secret Giraffic Jam. The sector wasn't wide—Noah could plainly see the blinking light marking the entrance into the City of Species about three hundred feet away. But what the sector lacked in width, it made up for in height. Through an endless vista of trees, walkways swerved and turned and dipped, like a tangle of roadways in a Dr. Seuss book. Autumn had brushed color across the magical heights, and leaves rained down and piled on everything—the walkways, the ground, even the branches. The giraffes, too numerous to count, paced in all directions on the winding decks, their powerful necks sweeping about. They reached their heads far over the rails, defeating the simple obstacle of distance to munch on leaves.

"Incredible," Richie muttered. With his face raised to take in the scene, his wiggly pom-pom dangled off his hat.

From above on the walkway, three people jogged up: Sam, Solana, and Hannah. They maneuvered through the giraffes, ducking beneath their outstretched necks and speckled bodies. They stepped up to the scouts and wordlessly stood there. As Tameron moved away to join his friends, the scouts traded nervous glances. The only sounds were the clomping of the giraffes' hooves and the occasional *pop* of Hannah's gum.

Sam fixed his eyes on Noah and finally said, "What are you trying to prove?" cracking each word like a whip.

Noah opened his mouth to speak, but his tongue simply sat between his teeth, spongy and shapeless.

"You got an answer?"

Noah knew he had to say something, so he released the first words his tongue managed to form. "I . . . I thought I could go in the Grottoes . . . and it would be no big deal. I thought—"

"Do you have any *clue* what you've done?" Sam turned to Megan. "And you! At what point did you think it'd be cool to ride your minibike across the zoo?"

Megan started to say something, but Noah interrupted her. "It's not her fault. It's mine."

Sam shook his head at Noah. "This was the most dangerous, most unnecessary stunt a Crosser has ever pulled! *Ever!* Are you *trying* to get the Secret Society discovered?"

"You're right," Noah conceded. "It was wrong—totally wrong." He stared at his feet. "I was confused. And looking for answers the wrong way."

"Let me tell you how it works," Sam said. "You learn what we want you to learn!"

"How are we supposed to help you if we don't understand everything that's going on? How can we be on your side if—"

"That's just it! You're not on our side, and you won't be—not ever. You're Outsiders. Don't you get it?"

Noah flushed with anger. "That doesn't mean anything!"

"Maybe not to you. But to us on the Inside, it makes all the difference in the world."

Noah turned to the other Descenders. Tameron stared down at the scouts, his eyes buried in the shadow of his hat brim. Hannah worked her jaw, perpetually reshaping the gum in her mouth. Solana stood with her shoulders slumped, her hip cocked to one side, the tips of her fingers tucked into her pants pockets.

Noah could think of nothing to say but the truth. "We might be Outsiders, but we're not going anywhere, not until this is done, not until the sasquatches are found and DeGraff is stopped. If DeGraff gets Inside, we're all in trouble, not just you guys, but us on the Outside. Our families, our friends. Don't you think that gives us a right to understand what's going on?"

The Descenders only hardened their stares.

"Look," Noah said. "I messed up. But . . ." He stumbled over his thoughts and added, "Why couldn't you just tell us about the Grottoes, huh? And why can't you just tell us who you are? Your jackets . . . your boots . . . they obviously have some kind of purpose. And those velvet patches—that's the same fabric as the curtains, right?"

Noah reached out to touch the velvet on Sam's shoulder, but he pulled away.

"*Descender*," Noah continued. "I looked that word up. A descender can be the part of a letter that drops below the rest of it. Do you know what I'm talking about? In the letter *y*, the descender would be the little slash"—he made a cutting motion with his fingertip—"that drops down. The descender is the tail on the body of a letter."

Hannah stopped chomping her gum and Solana uneasily shifted her stance. Ella, Richie, and Megan stared at Noah, waiting for more.

"The *tail* on the *body*," Noah repeated. "The *tail* on the *body* formed by two converging lines. The definition obviously refers to a line on a piece of paper, but couldn't the line be something else? A line of defense, maybe—like Tameron talked about. He talked about a line of animals and a line of humans guarding the Secret Zoo."

Tameron stepped forward. "Kid, are you nuts? We're not letters—we're people! You think you can pick up a dictionary and figure out—"

"If you guys only give us pieces of information, then we have to put those pieces together!" said Noah. All around him, falling leaves continued to pile on the deck. "It would make it a lot easier if you'd give us the complete picture instead."

No response.

Noah took a step forward. "You know what I think? I think the magic of this place has somehow changed you."

At this, Ella and Richie drew back from Noah. Megan gently laid her hand on her brother's shoulder.

"C'mon, Noah," she whispered to him. "You're getting a bit carried away, don't you think?"

Shrugging off his sister's hand, Noah looked straight at Sam and said, "Tell me I'm not just making this stuff up in my head."

Sam kept his stare locked on Noah's. Each refused to look away. The other scouts silently stood by.

"Noah," Megan said, "let it go. This isn't the time or—"

"When is the time? Huh? When the sasquatches rip apart the Secret Zoo? When DeGraff gets inside this stupid place? When is it going to be a good time for us to learn what we're dealing with?"

Sam took a step toward Noah. "You think we're just going to stand here and let you destroy us?"

"*Destroy* you?"

Megan squeezed between Sam and Noah. "Listen, bro," she coaxed. "You need to cool off. This is getting—"

Noah pulled away from the group and started pacing.

His face was flushed with anger, and his heart was pounding. Megan was right about one thing—he needed to cool down.

He walked to the edge of the deck. With his back to everyone, he leaned his forearms against the rail and stared out into the Secret Giraffic Jam. Throughout the sector, the giraffes had craned their long necks toward the commotion.

To Sam, Megan said, "Look, maybe we should—"

These were the last words Noah heard. All his attention was suddenly diverted to an intense pain that had sparked in the bottom of his left leg. He looked down to see a beastly hand clutching his ankle. From under the walkway, the yellow eyes of a sasquatch stared up at him.

The monster pulled Noah's leg, dragging him under the railing. Noah felt himself hurtling through space, then he thudded against the hard ground. Stars filled his vision. Dazed, he rolled onto his back, stirring the fallen leaves. The sasquatch lunged at him, its bladelike claws spread out like weapons.

It all happened so fast that Noah didn't have time to scream.

ᕫ CHAPTER 42 ᕫ

THE STRIKE OF THE SASQUATCH

As the sasquatch swung its claws down, Noah threw himself aside. The beast just missed him and ripped open the earth, slinging dirt into the air. Noah jumped up and took off running into the core of the sector. Glancing over his shoulder, he saw the sasquatch drop to all fours and chase after him, its rocky knuckles pounding the ground. In its wicked snarl, Noah saw two sets of fangs and a wall of huge square teeth.

Giraffes scattered. Their hooves kicked leaves into a low cloud of swirling colors that Noah charged through.

Noah ran upon a stream embedded about three feet in

the ground. He jumped down its steep bank and splashed into the water, which came to his knees, deeper than he'd expected. He plowed across it and leaped over the embankment on the opposite side, landing on his stomach. Before he could rise, the earth around him quaked as the legs of the sasquatch slammed down, one on either side of him. The beast had jumped the width of the river and landed directly over Noah.

With a sideways glance, Noah saw that the monster's feet were as large as Noah's entire torso. From its toes sprang claws—claws that reminded Noah of bladed tools used for farming. Curling and yellow, they dug into the earth.

Noah somehow threw his weight forward, jumping low over the ground like a frog. At the same moment, the sasquatch swiped its claws at him, just missing Noah but shredding his jacket. A cloud of insulated padding swirled out into the air. Noah jumped to his feet and once again ran as fast as he could, his heart pounding.

Around him, giraffes continued to scramble. One darted in front of Noah, accidentally tripping him with its long leg. Noah fell headfirst and slid through the leaves. Turning onto his back, he found the sasquatch once again towering over him. The beast threw back its head and roared, exposing the piercing points of its fangs. Then it balled its knuckles and hammered them against its chest, roaring, raining spit everywhere. Then, abruptly, it fell silent and stood still, staring directly at Noah. Its intention was clear.

Destruction.

Was this payback? Revenge? Did the sasquatch know who Noah was? Did it understand how the scouts had thwarted the sasquatches' escape from the Dark Lands on their first trip to the Secret Zoo?

It didn't matter. Not really. In seconds, the claws of the sasquatch would come down and end his life. Poised over Noah, the beast roared mightily once more and cocked an arm. Its outspread claws glinted in the sunlight. Just as Noah became certain he'd be ripped apart, the ground shook. Around him, four astounding creatures had dropped in. Noah stared. First they looked like people. Then animals. Then something in-between.

❦ CHAPTER 43 ❧

THE DESCENT

The sasquatch snapped its stare to the four beings surrounding it. Noah watched from the ground, more than once attempting to blink away his disbelief.

The Descenders. But they had changed.

Behind the sasquatch stood Sam, his long, unruly bangs across his eyes like a mask. He held his arms out to his sides, and from his leather sleeves hung layers of great silver feathers. Wings. They sprouted from his arms and across his back, extending far beyond his normal reach. Noah could only guess at their span. Twelve feet? Fifteen feet? Twenty feet? More? Draped around him, they blotted out the light, casting a single shadow across Noah and the sasquatch. Sunlight burst on their edges, making the Descender appear to glow.

On one side of the sasquatch was Tameron—or what had once been Tameron, anyway. Now his head, arms, and torso were covered in layered bands of armor, like those of an armadillo. His hat with the low brim had turned into a helmet, one that covered his entire head except for his eyes and jaw. None of these traits astonished Noah more than the one that lay partially coiled on the ground beside the Descender: a tail. As long as fifteen feet, it was covered in armored plates and studded with a jumble of spikes, their concentration heaviest at the end of the tail. It had dropped from inside Tameron's backpack, and was surely the thing Noah had seen moving inside the big canvas bag in Butterfly Nets.

Standing on the other side of the sasquatch was Hannah. She was as much as a foot taller than before. The soles of her boots, once only an inch or two thick, were now at least ten inches high. As she shifted her weight to one side, her rubbery-looking soles bulged outward and then sprang back into shape. The leather sides of the boots had thickened, giving additional support to her lower legs. Noah's gaze lifted to Hannah's face. Almost incredibly, she was still chomping her gum.

Last, Noah saw Solana standing just beyond his head.

Her jacket was covered in quills at least twelve inches long. They lay flat, their bottom halves black, their top halves ivory white. They were longest on the backs of her gloves, fifteen inches or more. As she stood there with her arms hanging down, the quills on her gloves reached beyond her knees like long claws.

The sasquatch, now on all fours, turned in a slow circle, studying its adversaries. It rolled back its head and let loose the call of a beast the Secret Society had come to fear. It pounded its fists against the ground, sending waves rippling through its long, mangy hair.

The Descenders braced themselves. Sam beat his long silver wings, stirring the air. Tameron huddled into the protection of his armor. Hannah rocked on the springy soles of her boots. Solana raised her quill-covered fists. The Descenders were ready to lunge forward—ready to "pounce upon . . . to attack with violence and suddenness."

Ready to descend.

Just then, Ella's voice rang out. "Noah! *Move!*"

Ella's cry startled the sasquatch long enough for Noah to squirm out from under it and crawl between Tameron and Solana. Realizing that its captive was escaping, the sasquatch swung at Noah. As its arm swept through the air, Solana lunged forward and sank her quills into it. The sasquatch threw back its head and howled.

The beast turned and ran, directly at Hannah. She

pushed off on her boots and leaped high into the air—five feet, ten feet, fifteen feet, more. As the creature passed beneath her, Tameron dropped his shoulder and charged, plowing into its back and slamming it to the ground. Without breaking his stride, Tameron swung his massive tail high in the air. Its heavy, multispiked tip flew around in a perfect arc and landed on the sasquatch, crushing it. Immediately, the beast went still. The Descenders had killed it.

The scouts rushed to Noah, who lay in the spill of leaves. Everything was completely surreal to him.

The Descenders eased up. Hannah popped her gum; Sam swept his bangs out of his eyes; Solana dropped her arms and relaxed her stance. Across the heights of the sector, giraffes craned their necks over the winding decks to stare down on the scene.

Noah stood. The four scouts huddled close together and stared with wide-eyed apprehension at the Descenders.

"You're . . ." Noah searched the fog of his confusion for the right words. "You're animals."

"Not hardly." Sam stepped forward, his long wings trailing behind him like a cape. "We're human." He pointed to Hannah's boots. "And when have you ever seen an animal with feet like that?"

"But your wings." Noah pointed to Tameron. "And his tail."

"We carry their abilities, the things that make them great. We don't—"

Sam swung his head back. A growl had come from behind him. Through the trees stepped another sasquatch. Then a second. A third, and a fourth. They crept forward with their shoulders slouched, their mangy hair swaying. Goopy lines of spit clung to their fangs.

All four Descenders turned. Then they spread out and prepared to fight.

CHAPTER 44

THE DESCENDERS

When the sasquatches closed to within thirty feet of the Descenders, Tameron jumped forward and turned in a circle. His tail swung low to the ground and swept the first sasquatch off its feet, slamming it to the ground and sending tremors through the earth. Tameron's tail continued to swing, but the other sasquatches jumped to avoid it.

Hannah sprang out of a crouched position and her boots shot her forward and up. More than ten feet in the air, she rolled her legs beneath her and landed her boot soles on the chest of a sasquatch. The beast sailed backward and slammed into a tall tree, bursting the trunk. The tree creaked and groaned and finally toppled to one side, smashing through a deck before slamming to the ground. The dazed sasquatch staggered to its feet, shook the confusion out of its head, then charged forward.

Solana struck next. She reached across her back, plucked a handful of quills from her jacket, and then pitched her arm around. The black-and-white barbs sailed through the air like a cluster of deadly blades and then peppered the front of a sasquatch. The beast roared and stumbled backward, clutching at its chest and tearing the barbs from its flesh.

Sam stroked his wings and launched into the air. He tightly circled a sasquatch and kicked its back, driving it to the ground.

The scouts stayed huddled close on their hands and knees. Noah looked up and saw countless giraffes staring down from the weave of sprawling decks. A sasquatch took a hit from Hannah's right boot, struck the ground, then slid up to the scouts on its stomach. It stopped just inches from their knees and looked up at them. Then it angrily spread its lips, revealing the fullness of its yellow fangs.

Noah saw that Hannah was battling another sasquatch, and the other Descenders didn't seem aware of the danger the scouts now faced.

"Guys," Noah said. *"Run!"*

The scouts jumped to their feet and took off toward the middle of the sector. The sasquatch tore after them on all fours, throwing its body forward like an ape.

"Faster!" Noah called out.

The four of them charged beneath a low deck and burst out on the other side. The sasquatch followed, its head skimming the overhead planks. As the scouts made a sharp turn around a tree, Richie lost his balance and tumbled to the ground. Noah, being the only one to see what had happened, stopped and turned back for his friend. He wrapped his arms around Richie and hoisted him to his feet.

"Go!" Noah said, snapping his arm toward the girls.

As Richie took off, Noah stood his ground and faced the sasquatch, which was less than ten feet away. He had to lure it away from Ritchie, who was too slow and clumsy to escape it.

The sasquatch dove at Noah, who jumped aside, narrowly eluding the deadly points of its claws. They both struck the ground, rolled, then jumped to their feet. Then they turned and faced each other, less than fifteen feet dividing them.

"Hey, ugly," Noah said.

The sasquatch growled and peeled back its lips. It hunkered low and rolled back its shoulders. Noah turned in the direction opposite his friends and ran.

He ran as fast as he could.

❧ CHAPTER 45 ❧

THE CHASE

Noah turned left, then right. He jumped a bush and dodged a tree. A giraffe bolted across his path, just missing him, but swatting his shoulder with the bushy tip of its tail. Noah looked back. The sasquatch, on all fours, was closing in again.

Noah neared the ivy-covered wall of the sector, which rose and disappeared behind the treetops and curling clusters of decks. Against the wall was a walkway. It began at the ground thirty feet to Noah's left, and like a spiral staircase, slowly ascended as it followed the wall.

Noah realized he'd never be able to outrun the

sasquatch—his only hope was to outmaneuver it. He turned right and ran beside the walkway, which was at least ten feet over his head.

A giraffe suddenly ran up beside him and matched his pace. Because of its thin, almost indiscernible legs, its massive body seemed to hover. Surprisingly fast and nimble, the giraffe drifted over to within an arm's length of Noah and swiftly dropped its head in front of him.

Noah knew what the giraffe wanted him to do—he just didn't know if he could do it. He sucked back a deep breath and readied himself. Then he reached out, grabbed onto the animal's knobby horns, and dove into the air, swinging one leg across the giraffe's tree-trunkish neck. The animal lifted its head and hoisted Noah twenty feet into the air. Bouncing around, Noah squeezed the horns and tightly wrapped his ankles in front of the giraffe.

He glanced back. The sasquatch was still slowly gaining ground.

"He's catching up!" Noah hollered.

The giraffe veered a few feet toward the wall and dipped its head to the edge of the deck. The wooden rails blurred past. The animal clearly wanted Noah to jump to the walkway.

"Are you nuts?" Noah bellowed.

The giraffe twitched its big ears against his wrists.

Noah turned again to the blur of the walkway. It didn't

seem possible. But then he noticed the small ledge in front of the railing. Could he reach out with both hands, grab a post, and have his momentum swing his feet up to the ledge?

He glanced back. The sasquatch was within five feet.

There wasn't time to think. Noah threw his arms out to his side. His hands painfully bounced off the railing before his fingers closed on a post. His legs swept off the giraffe's neck, arched into the air, and touched down on the ledge. He quickly stood and pitched himself over the rail, the wind gushing out of his lungs as he came down hard on the wood.

He lay on his back and stared above him. He started to breathe a sigh of relief, then stopped. Something had moved next to his head. He turned to see the sasquatch's hands wrapped around two posts. The beast ripped away a section of the railing and hurled it upward. Then it jumped, and the top half of its body landed on the open floor.

Noah rolled to his hands and knees. As the sasquatch squirmed onto the deck, Noah was abruptly swept high into the air. A giraffe had charged in from behind him, jabbed its neck through Noah's legs, and then raised its head, situating him on its body just as the other giraffe had done. Noah quickly grabbed its horns and wrapped his ankles together.

The giraffe followed the walkway, which inclined steeply as it veered away from the building wall. Noah stared down and realized they were at least thirty feet high. He saw the tops of shorter trees and their splotches of color. Through them, he spotted the Descenders battling the sasquatches. Sam was sweeping through the air, and Tameron was heaving his tail around, snapping branches. On the ground lay one sasquatch, unconscious or dead.

Noah looked back. The sasquatch was closing in on him once again. Five feet, four feet. It swiped its claws and just missed the giraffe's spotted rump.

"Do something!" Noah called out.

The giraffe swerved to the side of the walkway and, without breaking its stride, leaned its head out to where a web of ivy dangled. Noah grabbed on and allowed himself to be pulled into the air. He swung about ten feet out, passed over another platform, and dropped down to it. He landed on his feet and took off running. Within seconds, the planks shook and a thud sounded behind him. He glanced back to see the sasquatch still giving chase.

The new deck was especially crowded with giraffes. They ran in all directions, occasionally bumping into one another. Noah avoided their long legs and shot beneath their bodies.

As he dodged one giraffe, he tripped on its legs and crashed into a spot where two decks intersected. He rolled onto his back, the sasquatch lunged at him, its mouth an open snarl, its claws ready to strike. But as the sasquatch's arm came down, a giraffe charged in from the connecting walkway, swept its neck under the beast, and slung its massive body over the rail. The sasquatch swiped at the nothingness of the air and then plummeted at least forty feet to its certain death.

The giraffe lowered its head and softly nudged Noah's side with its long, bony snout.

"Th-thanks," Noah said.

The giraffe wriggled its ears and stared deeply into Noah's eyes. Then it raised its head and backed away, making room for him to stand.

Noah hauled himself to his feet and said, "The other Crossers . . . I need to help."

The giraffe stared back, silent as ever. Then it retreated a few more steps, allowing space for Noah to run.

CHAPTER 46
THE TRUTH

As Noah returned to the Descenders, he saw the other scouts. He fell into the arms of his friends, who hugged him all at the same time.

"What happened to the sasquatch?" Richie asked.

"He's gone" was all Noah said.

The scouts turned to the Descenders, who'd defeated the other sasquatches. The four teenagers looked completely surreal. Sam stepped close to Noah and stared at him.

"We're descendants of the families that were murdered during the Sasquatch Rebellion."

Though Noah had never heard of the Sasquatch Rebellion, he knew what Sam was referring to. When the scouts had first met Mr. Darby, the old man had mentioned an organized attack by the sasquatches on the Secret Society. The attack had killed hundreds and destroyed parts of the City of Species. The sasquatches that weren't killed in the battle were captured and imprisoned in a single sector—a sector that then slowly eroded into the Dark Lands. Mr. Darby had described the attack as the Secret Zoo's darkest moment.

Sam continued, "We're part of the Secret Zoo's army. The Secret Society trusts us to keep them safe from any threat, inside or out."

Megan said, "But there are only four of you."

Sam shook his head. "There are many more."

"What? How many more?"

"Enough that we inhabit an entire sector. The Sector of Descent. We live and train there."

Richie said, "But the others . . . we've never seen them." He paused to consider something. "Or have we?"

"Look . . . they shouldn't matter to you because it's the four of us who are responsible for your training. Why? Because we're Crossers. Our responsibility is the border of the Clarksville Zoo. The others safeguard the Inside— the City of Species and the other sectors."

"But why not just tell us that? Why—?"

"I just told you—it's our job to keep the Secret Society safe from any threat, inside or out."

"But you need—"

"Enough! I need to get a hold of Darby and Red and have them scour this sector for sasquatches." He turned to Hannah and said, "Get these kids out of here. If the cops are still in the Clarksville Zoo, hold them in the Grottoes until they're gone."

With a nod of her head and a pop of her gum, Hannah waved her hands at the scouts and started to walk off. Noah noticed that her boots had returned to normal. The scouts trailed her closely, each of them stunned and confused by the events that had just unfolded.

"You were right," Richie whispered to Noah so that Hannah couldn't hear. "About the Descenders."

Noah nodded.

"What about the Grottoes?" Megan whispered. "Did you get a good look at them?"

"You could say that," Noah answered.

"What did they—"

"We'll talk about it later."

Silence. As they walked, Noah turned to the sector. He searched its bright, colorful heights and thought about the Secret Zoo. He wondered about the Descenders and the way they had changed into something else. He imagined Kavita, her magic that the Great Pyramid still fed into the darkness of the world. He pondered the Grottoes and the wild way they joined the exhibits and other places across the Clarksville Zoo. He thought about the Shadowist, a strange being stalking this world.

Richie, apparently having the same thoughts as Noah, said, "This place is *beyond* amazing,"

"We haven't seen anything yet," Noah said.

"Huh?" Richie asked. "What do you mean?"

"Our adventure," Noah answered. "It's only begun."

Noah ignored the curious stares of his friends. No one dared to speak. The scouts followed Hannah up the deck toward the gateway that would take them home.

For now.

≈❧ CHAPTER 47 ❧≈
CHARLIE MAKES A DECISION

The scouts waited in the Grottoes for almost an hour until Hannah was able to confirm that the police had left. Then, after a guard locked visitors out of Giraffic Jam, the scouts crossed back fully to the Clarksville Zoo.

As the four friends walked to the exit of the zoo, keeping their heads down and their faces hidden, a man stepped out from his hiding place behind a concession stand. He had a mop of bright red hair, a splattering of freckles, and plump lips locked in a wicked snarl. Charlie Red. Watching the scouts from a distance, he shook his head and stood with his hands on his hips.

A staticky voice rose from the walkie-talkie clipped to his belt. "Charlie, they're out now. And they're headed this way." It was a security guard at the front gate. "You want us to stop them?"

Charlie thought about this for a moment. Then he unclipped the walkie-talkie and held it to his mouth. "No. Let them go."

"Roger."

Charlie fastened the walkie-talkie back on his hip. Then he turned and walked to the back of the zoo, away from the front gates. It wasn't time to stop the scouts.

Not yet.